My Name Is Aram

William Saroyan

Illustrated by Don Freeman

DOVER PUBLICATIONS
Garden City, New York

Copyright

Copyright © 1937, 1938, 1939, 1940, 1966, 1967 by William Saroyan
All rights reserved.

Bibliographical Note

This Dover edition, first published in 2013, is an unabridged republication of the work originally published as a Laurel Book by Bantam Doubleday Dell Publishing Group, New York, in 1991. The work was first published by Harcourt, Brace and Company, New York, in 1940. This Dover edition is published by arrangement with The Stanford University Libraries, managers of the literary estate of William Saroyan.

Library of Congress Cataloging-in-Publication Data

Saroyan, William, 1908–1981.
  My name is Aram / William Saroyan ; illustrated by Don Freeman.
    p. cm.
  ISBN-13: 978-0-486-49090-8
  ISBN-10: 0-486-49090-4
  I. Freeman, Don, 1908–1978. II. Title.

PS3537.A826M9 2013
813'.52—dc23

2012038905

Manufactured in the United States of America
49090414   2022
www.doverpublications.com

Contents

The Summer
of the Beautiful
White Horse

One day back there in the good old days when I was nine and the world was full of every imaginable kind of magnificence, and life was still a delightful and mysterious dream, my cousin Mourad, who was considered crazy by everybody who knew him except me, came to my house at four in the morning and woke me up by tapping on the window of my room.

Aram, he said.

I jumped out of bed and looked out the window.

I couldn't believe what I saw.

It wasn't morning yet, but it was summer and

with daybreak not many minutes around the corner of the world it was light enough for me to know I wasn't dreaming.

My cousin Mourad was sitting on a beautiful white horse.

I stuck my head out of the window and rubbed my eyes.

Yes, he said in Armenian. It's a horse. You're not dreaming. Make it quick if you want to ride.

I knew my cousin Mourad enjoyed being alive more than anybody else who had ever fallen into the world by mistake, but this was more than even I could believe.

In the first place, my earliest memories had been memories of horses and my first longings had been longings to ride.

This was the wonderful part.

In the second place, we were poor.

This was the part that wouldn't permit me to believe what I saw.

We were poor. We had no money. Our whole tribe was poverty-stricken. Every branch of the Garoghlanian family was living in the most amazing and comical poverty in the world. Nobody could understand where we ever got money enough to keep us with food in our bellies, not even the old men of the family. Most important of all, though, we were famous for our honesty. We had been famous for our honesty for something like eleven centuries, even when we had been the wealthiest family in what we liked to think was the world. We

were proud first, honest next, and after that we believed in right and wrong. None of us would take
advantage of anybody in the world, let alone steal.

Consequently, even though I could *see* the horse,
so magnificent; even though I could *smell* it, so
lovely; even though I could *hear* it breathing, so ex-
citing; I couldn't *believe* the horse had anything to
do with my cousin Mourad or with me or with any
of the other members of our family, asleep or
awake, because I *knew* my cousin Mourad couldn't
have *bought* the horse, and if he couldn't have
bought it he must have *stolen* it, and I refused to
believe he had stolen it.

No member of the Garoghlanian family could be
any kind of a thief, let alone a horse thief.

I stared first at my cousin and then at the horse.
There was a pious stillness and humor in each of
them which on the one hand delighted me and on
the other frightened me.

Mourad, I said, where did you steal this horse?

Leap out of the window, he said, if you want to
ride.

It was true, then. He *had* stolen the horse. There
was no question about it. He had come to invite me
to ride or not, as I chose.

Well, it seemed to me stealing a horse for a ride
was not the same thing as stealing something else,
such as money. For all I knew, maybe it wasn't
stealing at all. If you were crazy about horses the
way my cousin Mourad and I were, it wasn't stealing. It wouldn't become stealing until we offered to

sell the horse, which of course I knew we would never do.

Let me put on some clothes, I said.

All right, he said, but hurry.

I leaped into my clothes.

I jumped down to the yard from the window and leaped up onto the horse behind my cousin Mourad.

That year we lived at the edge of town, on Walnut Avenue. Behind our house was the country: vineyards, orchards, irrigation ditches, and country roads. In less than three minutes we were on Olive Avenue, and then the horse began to trot. The air was new and lovely to breathe. The feel of the horse running was wonderful. My cousin Mourad who was considered one of the craziest members of our family began to sing. I mean, he began to roar.

Every family has a crazy streak in it somewhere, and my cousin Mourad was considered the natural inheritor of the crazy streak in our tribe. Before him was our uncle Khosrove, an enormous man with a powerful head of black hair and the largest mustache in the San Joaquin Valley, a man so furious in temper, so irritable, so impatient that he stopped anyone from talking by roaring, *It is no harm; pay no attention to it.*

That was all, no matter what anybody happened to be talking about. Once it was his own son Arak running eight blocks to the barber shop where his father was having his mustache trimmed to tell him their house was on fire. This man Khosrove sat up in the chair and roared, It is no harm; pay no attention to it. The barber said, But the boy says your house is on fire. So Khosrove roared, Enough, it is no harm, I say.

My cousin Mourad was considered the descendant of this man, although Mourad's father was Zorab, who was practical and nothing else. That's how it was in our tribe. A man could be the father of his son's flesh, but that did not mean that he was also the father of his spirit. The distribution of the various kinds of spirit of our tribe had been from the beginning capricious and vagrant.

We rode and my cousin Mourad sang. For all anybody knew we were still in the old country where, at least according to some of our neighbors, we belonged. We let the horse run as long as it felt like running.

At last my cousin Mourad said, Get down. I want to ride alone.

Will you let me ride alone?

That is up to the horse.

The *horse* will let me ride.

We shall see. Don't forget that I have a way with a horse.

Well, any way you have with a horse, I have also.

For the sake of your safety, he said, let us hope so. Get down.

All right, I said, but remember you've got to let me try to ride alone.

I got down and my cousin Mourad kicked his heels into the horse and shouted, *Vazire*, run. The horse stood on its hind legs, snorted, and burst into a fury of speed that was the loveliest thing I had ever seen. My cousin Mourad raced the horse across a field of dry grass to an irrigation ditch, crossed the ditch on the horse, and five minutes later came back, dripping wet.

The sun was coming up, and so everything had bright light upon it, especially the horse.

Now it's my turn to ride, I said.

My cousin Mourad got off the horse.

Ride, he said.

I leaped to the back of the horse and for a moment knew the awfulest fear imaginable. The horse did not move.

Kick into his muscles, my cousin Mourad said. What are you waiting for? We've got to take him back before everybody in the world is up and about.

I kicked into the muscles of the horse. Once again it reared and snorted. Then it began to run. I didn't know what to do. Instead of running across the field to the irrigation ditch the horse ran down the road to the vineyard of Dikran Halabian where it began to leap over vines. The horse leaped over seven vines before I fell. Then it ran away.

My cousin Mourad came running down the road.

I'm not worried about you, he shouted. We've got to get that horse. You go this way and I'll go this way. If you come upon him, be kindly. I'll be near.

I ran down the road and my cousin Mourad ran across the field toward the irrigation ditch.

It took him half an hour to find the horse and bring him back.

All right, he said, jump on. The whole world is awake now.

What will we do? I said.

Well, he said, we'll either take him back or hide him until tomorrow morning.

He didn't sound worried and I knew he'd hide him and not take him back. Not for a while, at any rate.

Where will we hide him?

I know a place.

How long ago did you steal this horse? I said.

It suddenly dawned on me that he had been taking these early morning rides for some time and had come for me this morning only because he knew how much I longed to ride.

Who said anything about stealing a horse?

Anyhow, how long ago did you begin riding every morning?

Not until this morning.

Are you telling the truth?

Of course not, he said, but if we are found out, that's what you're to say. I don't want both of us to be liars. All you know is that we started riding this morning.

All right, I said.

He walked the horse quietly to the barn of a deserted vineyard which at one time had been the pride of a farmer named Vahan Fetvajian. There were some oats and dry alfalfa in the barn.

We began walking home.

It wasn't easy, he said, to get the horse to behave so nicely. At first it wanted to run wild, but, as I've told you, I have a way with a horse. I can get it to want to do anything *I* want it to do. Horses understand me.

How do you do it? I said.

I have an understanding with a horse.

Yes, but what kind of an understanding?

A simple and honest one.

Well, I wish I knew how to reach an understanding like that with a horse.

You're still a small boy, he said. When you get to be thirteen you'll know how to do it.

I went home and ate a hearty breakfast.

That afternoon my uncle Khosrove came to our house for coffee and cigarettes. He sat in the parlor, sipping and smoking and remembering the old country. Then another visitor arrived, a farmer named John Byro, an Assyrian who, out of loneliness, had learned to speak Armenian. My mother brought the lonely visitor coffee and tobacco and he rolled a cigarette and sipped and smoked, and then at last, sighing sadly, he said, My white horse which was stolen last month is still gone. I cannot understand it.

My uncle Khosrove became very irritated and shouted, It's no harm. What is the loss of a horse? Haven't we all lost the homeland? What is this crying over a horse?

That may be all right for you, a city dweller, to

say, but what about my surrey? What good is a surrey without a horse?

Pay no attention to it, my uncle Khosrove roared. I walked ten miles to get here.

You have legs.

My left leg pains me.

Pay no attention to it.

That horse cost me sixty dollars, John Byro said.

I spit on money, my uncle Khosrove said.

He got up and stalked out of the house, slamming the screen door.

My mother explained.

He has a gentle heart, she said. It is simply that he is homesick and such a large man.

The farmer went away and I ran over to my cousin Mourad's house.

He was sitting under a peach tree, repairing the hurt wing of a young robin which could not fly. He was talking to the bird.

What is it? he said.

The farmer, John Byro. He visited our house. He wants his horse. You've had it a month. I want you to promise not to take it back until I learn to ride.

It will take you a *year* to learn to ride.

We could keep the horse a year.

My cousin Mourad leaped to his feet.

What? he roared. Are you inviting a member of the Garoghlanian family to steal? The horse must go back to its true owner.

When?

In six months at the latest.

He threw the bird into the air. The bird tried hard, almost fell twice, but at last flew away, high and straight.

Early every morning for two weeks my cousin Mourad and I took the horse out of the barn of the deserted vineyard where we were hiding it and rode it, and every morning the horse, when it was my turn to ride alone, leaped over grape vines and small trees and threw me and ran away. Nevertheless, I hoped in time to learn to ride the way my cousin Mourad rode.

One morning on our way to Vahan Fetvajian's deserted vineyard we ran into the farmer John Byro who was on his way to town.

Let me do the talking, my cousin Mourad said. I have a way with farmers.

Good morning, John Byro, my cousin Mourad said to the farmer.

The farmer studied the horse eagerly.

Good morning, sons of my friends, he said. What is the name of your horse?

My Heart, my cousin Mourad said in Armenian.

A lovely name for a lovely horse. I could swear it is the horse that was stolen from me many weeks ago. May I look into its mouth?

Of course, Mourad said.

The farmer looked into the mouth of the horse.

Tooth for tooth, he said. I would swear it *is* my horse if I didn't know your parents. The fame of your family for honesty is well known to me. Yet the horse is the twin of my horse. A suspicious man

THE BEAUTIFUL WHITE HORSE   11

would believe his eyes instead of his heart. Good day, my young friends.

Good day, John Byro, my cousin Mourad said.

Early the following morning we took the horse to John Byro's vineyard and put it in the barn. The dogs followed us around without making a sound.

The dogs, I whispered to my cousin Mourad. I thought they would bark.

They would at somebody else, he said. I have a way with dogs.

My cousin Mourad put his arms around the horse, pressed his nose into the horse's nose, patted it, and then we went away.

That afternoon John Byro came to our house in his surrey and showed my mother the horse that had been stolen and returned.

I do not know what to think, he said. The horse is stronger than ever. Better-tempered, too. I thank God.

My uncle Khosrove, who was out of sight in the parlor, suddenly shouted, Quiet, man, quiet. Your horse has been returned. Pay no attention to it.

The Journey to Hanford

The time came one year for my sad uncle Jorgi to fix his bicycle and ride twenty-seven miles to Hanford, where it seems there was a job. I went with him, although at first there was talk of sending my cousin Vask instead.

The family didn't want to complain about having among its members a fool like Jorgi, but at the same time it wanted a chance, in the summertime, to forget him for a while. If he went away and got himself a job in Hanford, in the watermelons, all would be well. Jorgi would earn a little money and at the same time be out of the way. That was the important thing—to get him out of the way.

To hell with him and his zither both, my grandfather said. When you read in a book that a man who sits all day under a tree and plays a zither and sings is a great man, believe me, that writer is a liar. Money, that's the thing. Let him go and sweat under the sun for a while. Him and his zither both.

You say that now, my grandmother said, but wait a week. Wait till you need music again.

That is nonsense, my grandfather said. Let him go. It is twenty-seven miles to Hanford. That is a good intelligent distance.

You speak that way *now*, my grandmother said, but in three days you'll be a melancholy man. I shall see you walking about like a tiger. I am the one who shall see that. Seeing that, I am the one who shall laugh.

You are a woman, my grandfather said. When you read in a book with hundreds of pages of small print that a woman is truly a creature of wonder, that writer has turned his face away from his wife and is dreaming. Let him go.

It is simply that you are not young any longer, my grandmother said. That is the thing that is making you roar.

Close your mouth, my grandfather said. Close it, or here comes the back of my hand.

My grandfather looked about the room at his children and grandchildren.

I say he goes to Hanford on his bicycle. What do you say?

Nobody spoke.

Then that's settled, my grandfather said. Now, who shall we send with him? Which of the uncouth of our children shall we punish by sending him with Jorgi to Hanford? When you read in a book that a journey to another city is a pleasant experience for a young man, that writer is probably a man of eighty or ninety who as a child once went in a wagon two miles from home. Who shall we punish? Vask? Shall Vask be the one? Step up here, boy.

My cousin Vask got up from the floor and stood in front of the old man, who looked down at him furiously, twisted his enormous mustaches, cleared his throat, and put his hand over the boy's face. His hand practically covered the whole head. Vask didn't move.

Shall you go with your uncle Jorgi to Hanford? my grandfather said.

If it pleases my grandfather, Vask said.

The old man began to make faces, thinking it over.

Let me think a moment, he said. Jorgi's spirit is the foolish one of our tribe. Yours is also. Is it wise to put two fools together?

He turned to the others.

Let me hear your thoughts on this theme. Is it wise to put a grown fool and a growing one to-

gether, of the same tribe? Will it profit anyone?
Speak up, so I may consider.

I think it would be the natural thing to do, my
uncle Zorab said. A fool and a fool. The man to
work, the boy to keep house and cook.

Perhaps, my grandfather said. Let's consider. A
fool and a fool, one to work, the other to keep house
and cook. Can you cook, boy?

Of course he can cook, my grandmother said.
Rice, at least.

Is that true, boy, about the rice? Two cups of water, one cup of rice, one teaspoonful of salt. Do you
know about the trick of making it come out like
food instead of swill?

Of course he can cook rice, my grandmother said.

The back of my hand is on its way to your mouth,
my grandfather said. Let the boy speak for himself.
He has a tongue. Can you do it, boy? When you
read in a book that a boy answers an old man
wisely, that writer has read the Old Testament and
is bent on exaggeration. Can you make it come out
like food, not swill?

I have cooked rice, Vask said. It came out like
food.

Was there enough salt to it? If you lie, remember
my hand.

Vask hesitated a moment.

I understand, my grandfather said. You are embarrassed about the rice. What was wrong with it?
Truth is all that pleases me. Speak up fearlessly. If it

is the truth fearlessly, no man can demand more. What embarrasses you about the rice?

It was too salty, Vask said. We had to drink water all day and all night.

No elaboration, my grandfather said. Only what is true. The rice was too salty. Naturally you had to drink water all day and all night. We've all eaten that kind of rice. Don't think because you drank water all day and all night that you are the first Armenian who ever did that. Just tell me that it was too salty. I'm not here to learn. I *know*. Just say it was too salty and let me try to determine if you are the one to go.

My grandfather turned to the others. He began to make faces again.

I think this is the boy to go, he said, but speak up, if you have something to say. Salty is better than swill. Was it light in texture, boy?

It was light in texture, Vask said.

I believe this is the one to send, my grandfather said. The water is good for the gut. Shall it be this boy, Vask Garoghlanian, or who?

On second thought, my uncle Zorab said, two fools, out and out, perhaps not, although the rice is not swill. I nominate Aram. Perhaps he should go. He deserves to be punished.

Everybody looked at me.

Aram? my grandfather said. Our Aram?

Who else would he mean? my grandmother said. You know very well who he means.

My grandfather turned slowly and for half a minute looked at my grandmother.

When you read in a book about some man who falls in love with a girl and marries her, that writer is a very young man who has no idea she is going to talk out of turn right up to the time she is ready to go into the ground at the age of ninety-seven.

Aram *Garoghlanian?* he said.

Yes, my uncle Zorab said.

What has he done to deserve this awful punishment?

He knows.

Aram Garoghlanian, my grandfather said.

I got up and stood in front of my grandfather. He put his big hand over my face and rubbed it.

What have you done? he said.

Which one? I said.

My grandfather turned to my uncle Zorab.

Tell the boy which mischief to acknowledge. There appear to be several.

He knows which one, my uncle Zorab said.

Do you mean showing the neighbors how you pick your teeth? Using one hand to hide the work of the other.

My uncle Zorab refused to speak.

Or do you mean walking and talking the way you walk and talk?

This is the boy to send with Jorgi, my uncle Zorab said.

Can you cook rice? my grandfather said.

He didn't care to go into detail about my making

fun of my uncle Zorab. If I could cook rice, I should go with Jorgi to Hanford. That was what it came to. Of course I *wanted* to go, no matter what the writer was who wrote that it was a fine experience for a boy to travel. Fool or liar or anything else, I *wanted* to go.

I can cook rice, I said.

Salty or swill, or what?

Sometimes salty. Sometimes swill. Sometimes perfect.

Let's consider, my grandfather said.

He leaned against the wall, considering.

Three large glasses of water, he said to my grandmother.

My grandmother went to the kitchen and after a moment returned with three large glasses of water on a tray. My grandfather drank one glass after another, then turned to the others, making many thoughtful faces.

Sometimes salty, he said. Sometimes swill. Sometimes perfect. Is this the boy to send to Hanford?

Yes, my uncle Zorab said. The only one.

So be it, my grandfather said. That will be all. I wish to be alone.

I moved to go. My grandfather took me by the neck.

Stay a moment, he said.

When we were alone he said, Walk and talk the way your uncle Zorab walks and talks.

I did so and my grandfather roared with laughter.

Go to Hanford, he said. Go with the fool Jorgi and make it salty or make it swill or make it perfect.

In this manner I was assigned to be my uncle Jorgi's companion on his journey to Hanford.

We set out the following morning before daybreak. I sat on the crossbar of the bicycle and my uncle Jorgi on the seat, but when I got tired I got off and walked, and after a while my uncle Jorgi got off and walked, and I rode. We didn't reach Hanford until late that afternoon.

We were supposed to stay in Hanford till the job ended, after the watermelon season. That was the idea. We went around town looking for a house to stay in, a house with a stove in it, gas connections, and water. We didn't care about electricity, but we wanted gas and water. We saw six or seven houses and then we saw one my uncle Jorgi liked, so we moved in that night. It was an eleven-room house, with a gas stove, a sink with running water, and a room with a bed and a couch. The other rooms were all empty. My uncle Jorgi lighted a candle, brought out his zither, sat on the floor, and began to play and sing. It was beautiful. It was melancholy sometimes and sometimes funny, but it was always beautiful. I don't know how long he played and sang before he realized he was hungry, but all of a sudden he got up off the floor and said, Aram, I want rice.

I made a pot of rice that night that was both salty and swill, but my uncle Jorgi said, Aram, this is wonderful.

The birds got us up at daybreak.

The job, I said. You begin today, you know.

Today, my uncle Jorgi groaned.

He walked out of the empty house and I looked around for a broom. There was no broom, so I went out and sat on the steps of the front porch. It seemed to be a nice region of the world in daylight. It was a street with only four houses. There was a church steeple in front of the house, two blocks away. I sat on the porch about an hour. My uncle Jorgi came up the street, on his bicycle, zigzagging with joy unconfined.

Not this year, thank God, he said.

What?

There is no job, thank our Heavenly Father.

Why not?

The season is over.

That isn't true.

The season is over, finished, concluded.

Your father will break your head.

Praise God, the watermelons are all harvested.

Who said so?

The farmer himself.

He just said that. He didn't want to hurt your feelings. He just said that because he knew your heart wouldn't be in your work.

Praise God, the whole season is over. All the fine, ripe watermelons have been harvested.

What are we going to do? The season is just beginning.

It's ended. We shall dwell in this house a month

and then go home. We have paid six dollars rent and we have money enough for rice. We shall rest here a month and then go home.

With no money, I said.

But in good health, he said. Praise God, who ripened them so early this year.

My uncle Jorgi danced into the house to his zither, and before I could decide what to do about him he was playing and singing. It was so beautiful I didn't even get up and try to chase him out of the house. I just sat on the porch and listened.

We stayed in the house a month and then went home. My grandmother was the first to see us.

It's about time you two came home, she said. He's been raging like a tiger. Give me the money.

There is no money, I said.

Did he work?

No. He played and sang the whole month.

How did your rice turn out?

Sometimes salty. Sometimes swill. Sometimes perfect. But he didn't work.

His father mustn't know. I have money.

She lifted her dress and got some currency out of a pocket in her pants and put it in my hands.

When he comes home, give him this money.

She looked at me a moment, then added: *Aram Garoghlanian.*

I will do as you say.

When my grandfather came home he began to roar.

Home already? Is the season ended so soon? Where is the money he earned?

I gave him the money.

I won't have him singing all day, my grandfather roared. There is a limit to everything. When you read in a book that a father loves a foolish son more than his wise sons, that writer is a bachelor.

In the yard, under the almond tree, my uncle Jorgi began to play and sing. My grandfather came to a dead halt and began to listen. He sat down on the couch, took off his shoes, and began to make faces.

I went into the kitchen to get three or four glasses of water to quench the thirst from last night's rice. When I came back to the parlor the old man was stretched out on the couch, asleep and smiling, and his son Jorgi was singing hallelujah to the universe at the top of his beautiful, melancholy voice.

The Pomegranate Trees

My uncle Melik was just about the worst farmer that ever lived. He was too imaginative for his own good. What he wanted was beauty. He wanted to plant it and see it grow. I myself planted more than a hundred pomegranate trees. I drove a John Deere tractor, too, and so did my uncle. It was all art, not agriculture. My uncle just liked the idea of planting trees and watching them grow.

Only they wouldn't grow. It was on account of

the soil. The soil was desert soil. It was dry. My uncle waved at the six hundred and forty acres of desert he had bought and he said in the most poetic Armenian anybody ever heard, Here in this awful desolation a garden shall flower, fountains of cold water shall bubble out of the earth, and all things of beauty shall come into being.

Yes sir, I said.

I was the first and only member of the family to see the land. He knew I would understand the impulse that was driving him to ruin. I did. I knew as well as he that what he had bought was worthless desert land. It was away over to hell and gone, at the foot of the Sierra Nevada Mountains. It was full of every kind of desert plant that ever sprang out of dry hot earth. It was overrun with prairie dogs, squirrels, horned toads, snakes, and a variety of smaller forms of life. The space over this land knew only the presence of hawks, eagles, and buzzards. It was a region of silence, loneliness, emptiness, truth, and dignity. It was nature at its proudest, dryest, and loveliest.

My uncle and I got out of the Ford roadster and began to walk over the dry earth.

This land is my land, he said.

He walked slowly, kicking into the dry soil. A horned toad scrambled over the earth at my uncle's feet. My uncle clutched my shoulder and came to a halt.

What is that animal?

That little tiny lizard?

Yes. What is it?

I don't know for sure, but we call them horny toads.

The horned toad came to a halt about three feet away and turned its head.

My uncle looked down at the small animal.

Is it poison? he said.

To eat? Or if it bites you?

Either way.

I don't think it's good to eat. I think it's harmless. I've caught many of them. They grow sad in captivity, but never bite. Shall I catch this one?

Please do.

I sneaked up on the horned toad, then sprang on it while my uncle looked on.

Careful, he said. Are you sure it isn't poison?

I've caught many of them.

I took the horned toad to my uncle. He tried not to seem afraid.

A lovely little thing, isn't it? His voice was unsteady.

Would you like to hold it?

No. You hold it. I have never before been so close to such a thing as this. I see it has eyes. I suppose it can see us.

It's looking up at you right now.

My uncle looked the horned toad straight in the eye. The horned toad looked my uncle straight in the eye. For fully half a minute they looked one another straight in the eye and then the horned toad turned its head aside and looked down at the ground. My uncle sighed with relief.

A thousand of them, he said, could kill a man, I suppose.

They never travel in great numbers. You hardly ever see more than one at a time.

A big one could probably bite a man to death.

They don't grow big. This is as big as they get.

They seem to have an awful eye for such small creatures. Are you sure they don't mind being picked up?

They forget all about it the minute you put them down.

Do you really think so?

I don't think they have very good memories.

My uncle straightened up, breathing deeply.

Put the little creature down, he said. Let us be kind to the innocent inventions of Almighty God. If it is not poison and grows no larger than a mouse and does not travel in great numbers and has no memory to speak of, let the timid little thing return to the earth. Let us love these small things which live on the earth with us.

Yes sir.

I placed the horned toad on the ground.

Gently now. Let no harm come to this strange dweller on my land.

The horned toad scrambled away.

These little things have been living on soil of this kind for centuries, I said.

Centuries? my uncle said. Are you sure?

No, I'm not, but I imagine they have. They're still here, at any rate.

My uncle looked around at his land, at the cactus and brush growing out of it, at the sky overhead.

What have they been *eating* all this time? he said.

Insects, I guess.

What kind of insects?

Little bugs.

We continued to walk over the dry land. When we came to some holes in the earth my uncle stood over them and said, Who lives down there?

Prairie dogs.

What are *they?*

Well, they're something like rats. They belong to the rodent family.

What are all these things *doing* on my land?

They don't know it's your land. They're living here the same as ever.

I don't suppose that horny toad ever looked a man in the eye before.

I don't *think* so.

Do you think I scared it or anything?

I don't know for sure.

If I did, I didn't mean to. I'm going to build a house here some day.

I didn't know that.

I'm going to build a magnificent house.

It's pretty far away.

It's only an hour from town.

If you go fifty miles an hour.

It's not fifty miles to town. It's thirty-seven.

Well, you've got to take a little time out for rough roads.

I'll build me the finest house in the world. What else lives on this land?

Well, there are three or four kinds of snakes.

Poison or non-poison?

Mostly non. The rattlesnake is poison, though.

Do you mean to tell me there are *rattlesnakes* on this land?

This is the kind of land rattlesnakes *usually* live on.

How many?

Per acre? Or on the whole six hundred and forty acres?

Per acre.

Well, I'd say there are about three per acre, conservatively.

Three per acre? *Conservatively?*

Maybe only two.

How many is that to the whole place?

Well, let's see. Two per acre. Six hundred and forty acres. About fifteen hundred of them.

Fifteen hundred rattlesnakes?

An acre is pretty big. Two rattlesnakes per acre isn't many. You don't often see them.

What else have we got around here that's poison?

I don't know of anything else. All the other things are harmless. The rattlesnakes are harmless too, unless you step on them.

All right, my uncle said. You walk ahead and

watch where you're going. If you see a rattlesnake, don't step on it. I don't want you to die at the age of eleven.

Yes sir. I'll watch carefully.

We turned around and walked back to the Ford. I didn't see any rattlesnakes on the way. We got into the car and my uncle lighted a cigarette.

I'm going to make a garden in this awful desolation.

Yes sir.

I know what my problems are, and I know how to solve them.

How?

Do you mean the horny toads or the rattlesnakes?

I mean the problems.

Well, the first thing I'm going to do is hire some Mexicans and put them to work.

Doing what?

Clearing the land. Then I'm going to have them dig for water.

Dig where?

Straight down. After we get water, I'm going to have them plow the land, and then I'm going to plant.

Wheat?

Wheat? my uncle shouted. What do I want with wheat? Bread is five cents a loaf. I'm going to plant pomegranate trees.

How much are pomegranates?

Who knows? They're practically unknown in this country. Ten, fifteen, maybe twenty cents each.

Is that all you're going to plant?

I have in mind planting several other kinds of trees.

Peach?

About ten acres.

How about apricots?

By all means. The apricot is a lovely fruit. Lovely in shape, with a glorious flavor and a most delightful pit. I shall plant about twenty acres of apricot trees.

I hope the Mexicans don't have any trouble finding water. *Is* there water under this land?

Of course, my uncle said. The important thing is to get started. I shall instruct the men to watch out for rattlesnakes. Pomegranates. Peaches. Apricots. What else?

Figs?

Thirty acres of figs.

How about mulberries?

The mulberry is a very nice-looking tree, my uncle said. A tree I knew well in the old country. How many acres would you suggest?

About ten?

All right. What else?

Olive trees are nice.

Yes, they are. About ten acres of olive trees. Anything else?

Well, I don't suppose apple trees would grow on this kind of land.

No, but I don't like apples anyway.

He started the car and we drove off the dry land

on to the dry road. The car bounced about slowly until we reached the road and then we began to travel at a higher rate of speed.

One thing, my uncle said. When we get home I would rather you didn't mention this *farm* to the folks.

Yes sir. (*Farm?* I thought. *What farm?*)

I want to surprise them. You know how your grandmother is. I'll go ahead with my plans and when everything is in order I'll take the whole family out to the farm and surprise them.

Yes sir.

Not a word to a living soul.

Yes sir.

Well, the Mexicans went to work and cleared the land. They cleared about ten acres of it in about two months. There were seven of them. They worked with shovels and hoes. They didn't understand anything about anything. It all seemed very strange, but they never complained. They were being paid and that was the thing that counted. They were two brothers and their sons. One day the older brother, Diego, very politely asked my uncle what it was they were supposed to be doing.

Señor, he said, please forgive me. Why are we cutting down the cactus?

I'm going to farm this land, my uncle said.

The other Mexicans asked Diego in Mexican what my uncle had said and Diego told them.

They didn't believe it was worth the trouble to

tell my uncle he couldn't do it. They just went on cutting down the cactus.

The cactus, however, stayed down only for a short while. The land which had been first cleared was soon rich again with fresh cactus and brush. My uncle made this observation with considerable amazement.

Maybe it takes deep plowing to get rid of cactus, I said. Maybe you've got to *plow* it out.

My uncle talked the matter over with Ryan, who had a farm-implement business. Ryan told him not to fool with horses. The modern thing to do was to turn a good tractor loose on the land and do a year's work in a day.

So my uncle bought a John Deere tractor. It was beautiful. A mechanic from Ryan's taught Diego how to operate the tractor, and the next day when my uncle and I reached the land we could see the tractor away out in the desolation and we could hear it booming in the grand silence of the desert. It sounded crazy. It *was* crazy. My uncle thought it was wonderful.

Progress, he said. There's the modern age for you. Ten thousand years ago it would have taken a hundred men a week to do what the tractor has already done today.

Ten thousand years ago? You mean yesterday.

Anyway, there's nothing like these modern conveniences.

The tractor isn't a convenience.

What is it, then? my uncle said. Doesn't the driver sit?

He couldn't very well stand.

Any time they let you sit, it's a convenience. Can you whistle?

Yes sir. What kind of a song would you like to hear?

I don't want to hear any song. Whistle at the Mexican on the tractor.

What for?

Never mind what for. Just whistle. I want him to know we are here and that we are pleased with his work. He's probably plowed twenty acres.

Yes sir.

I put the second and third fingers of each hand into my mouth and blew with all my might. It was good and loud. Nevertheless, it didn't seem as if Diego had heard me. He was pretty far away. We were walking toward him anyway, so I couldn't figure out why my uncle wanted me to whistle at him.

Once again, he said.

I whistled once again, but again Diego didn't hear.

Louder, please.

This next time I gave it all I had, and my uncle put his hands over his ears. My face got red, but this time the Mexican on the tractor heard the whistle. He slowed the tractor down, turned it around, and began plowing straight across the field toward us.

Do you want him to do that?

It doesn't matter.

In less than a minute and a half the tractor and the Mexican arrived. The Mexican was delighted. He wiped dirt and perspiration off his face and got down from the tractor.

Señor, he said, this is wonderful.

I'm glad you like it, my uncle said.

Would you like a ride?

My uncle was sure he didn't. He looked at me.

Go ahead, he said. Hop on. Have a little ride.

Diego got on the tractor and helped me on. He sat on the metal seat and I stood behind him, holding him. The tractor began to shake, then jumped, and then began to go. The Mexican drove around in a big circle and brought the tractor back to my uncle. I jumped off.

All right, my uncle said to the Mexican. Go back to your work.

The Mexican drove the tractor back to where he was plowing.

My uncle didn't get water out of the land until many months later. He had wells dug all over the place, but no water came out of them. He had motor pumps installed, but even then no water came out. A water specialist named Roy came out from Texas with his two younger brothers and they began to investigate the land. At last they told my uncle they'd get water for him. It took them three months, but the water was muddy and there wasn't much of it. The specialist told my uncle matters would improve with time and went back to Texas.

Now half the land was cleared and plowed and there was water, so the time had come to plant.

We planted pomegranate trees. They were of the finest quality and very expensive. Altogether we planted about seven hundred of them, and I myself planted a hundred, while my uncle planted eight or nine. We had a twenty-acre orchard of pomegranate trees away over in the middle of the dry desert, and my uncle was crazy about it. The only trouble was, his money was running out. Instead of going ahead and trying to make a garden of the whole six hundred and forty acres, he decided to devote his time and energy and money to the pomegranate trees alone.

Only for the time being, he said. Until we begin to sell the pomegranates and get our money back.

Yes sir.

I didn't know for sure, but it seemed to me we wouldn't be getting any pomegranates to speak of from the little trees for two or three years at least, but I didn't say anything. My uncle got rid of the Mexican workers and he and I took over the farm. We had the tractor and a lot of land, so every now and then we drove out to the land and drove the tractor around, plowing up cactus and turning over the soil between the pomegranate trees.

The water situation didn't improve with time, however. Every once in a while there would be a sudden generous spurt of water containing only a few pebbles and my uncle would be greatly pleased, but the next day the water would be muddy again and there would be only a little trickle. The trees took root and held fast, but they just weren't getting enough water.

There were blossoms after the second year. This was a great triumph for my uncle, but nothing much ever came of the blossoms. They were beautiful, but that was about all.

That year my uncle harvested three small pomegranates.

I ate one, he ate one, and we kept the other one up in his office.

The following year I was fourteen. A number of good things had happened to me: I had discovered writing, and I'd grown as tall as my uncle. The pomegranate trees were still our secret. They had cost my uncle a lot of money, but he was always under the impression that very soon he was going to start marketing a big crop and get his money back and go on with his plan to make a garden in the desert.

The trees grew a little, but it was hardly noticeable. Quite a few of them withered and died.

That's average, my uncle said. Twenty trees to an acre is only average. We won't plant new trees just now. We'll do that later.

He was still paying for the land, too.

The following year we harvested about two hundred pomegranates. We packed them in nice-look-

ing boxes and my uncle shipped them to a wholesale produce house in Chicago. Eleven boxes.

We didn't hear from the wholesale produce house
for a month, so one night my uncle made a long-
distance phone call. The produce man, D'Agostino,
told my uncle nobody wanted pomegranates.

How much are you asking per box? my uncle
shouted over the phone.

One dollar, D'Agostino shouted back.

That's not enough, my uncle shouted. I won't
take a nickel less than five dollars a box.

They don't want them at one dollar a box,
D'Agostino shouted.

Why not? my uncle shouted.

They don't know what they are, D'Agostino
shouted.

What kind of a business man are you? my uncle
shouted. They're pomegranates. I want five dollars a
box.

I can't sell them, the produce man shouted. I ate
one myself and I don't see anything so wonderful
about them.

You're crazy, my uncle shouted. There is no other
fruit in the world like the pomegranate. Five dollars
a box isn't half enough.

What shall I do with them? D'Agostino shouted. I
can't sell them. I don't want them.

I see, my uncle whispered. Ship them back. Ship
them back express collect.

So the eleven boxes came back.

All winter my uncle and I ate pomegranates in our spare time.

The following year my uncle couldn't make any more payments on the land. He gave the papers back to the man who had sold him the land. I was in the office at the time.

Mr. Griffith, my uncle said, I've got to give you back your property, but I would like to ask a little favor. I've planted twenty acres of pomegranate trees out there on that land and I'd appreciate it very much if you'd let me take care of those trees.

Take care of them? Mr. Griffith said. What in the world for?

My uncle tried to explain, but couldn't. It was too much to try to explain to a man who wasn't sympathetic.

So my uncle lost the land, and the trees, too.

A few years later he and I drove out to the land and walked out to the pomegranate orchard. The trees were all dead. The soil was heavy again with cactus and desert brush. Except for the small dead pomegranate trees the place was exactly the way it had been all the years of the world.

We walked around in the dead orchard for a while and then went back to the car.

We got into the car and drove back to town.

We didn't say anything because there was such an awful lot to say, and no language to say it in.

One of
Our Future Poets,
You Might Say

W hen I was in the third grade at Emerson School, the Board of Education took a day off one day to think things over.

I was eight going on nine or at the most nine going on ten, and good-natured.

In those days the average Board of Education didn't make a fuss over the children of a small town and if some of the children seemed to be dumb, the average Board of Education assumed that this was natural and let it go at that.

Certain Presbyterian preachers, however, sometimes looked into a sea of young faces and said: You are the future leaders of America, the future captains of industry, the future statesmen, and, I might say, the future poets. This sort of talk always pleased me because I liked to imagine what kind of future captains of industry pals of mine like Al Vittore, Dick Basmaj, and Frankie Azevedo were going to be.

These boys were great baseball players, but by nature easy-going: healthy, strong, and simple. If they were asked what career they intended to shape for themselves, they would honestly say, I don't know; nothing, I guess.

According to documentary theory, published and tabulated, all the inhabitants of my neighborhood should have had badly shaped heads, sunken chests, faulty bone structure, hollow voices, no energy, distemper, and six or seven other minor organic defects.

According to the evidence before each public school teacher, however, these ruffians from the slums had well-shaped heads, sound chests, handsome figures, loud voices, too much energy, and a continuous compulsion to behave mischievously.

Something was wrong somewhere.

Our Board of Education decided to try to find out what.

They *did* find out.

They found out that the published and tabulated documentary theory was wrong.

It was at this time that I first learned with joy and fury that I was a poet. I remember being in the Civic Auditorium at high noon with six hundred other future statesmen, and I remember hearing my name on the alphabetical roll call sung out by old Miss Ogilvie in a clear hysterical soprano.

The time had arrived for me to climb the seventeen steps to the stage, walk to the center, strip to the waist, inhale, exhale, and be measured all over.

There was a moment of confusion and indecision, followed quickly by a superhuman impulse to behave with style, which I did, to the horror and bewilderment of the whole Board of Education, three elderly doctors, a half-dozen registered nurses, and six hundred future captains of industry.

Instead of climbing the seventeen steps to the stage, I *leaped.*

I remember old Miss Ogilvie turning to Mr. Rickenbacker, Superintendent of Public Schools, and whispering fearfully: This is Aram Garoghlanian— one of our future poets, I might say.

Mr. Rickenbacker took one quick look and whispered back: Who's he sore at?

Society, old Miss Ogilvie said.

So am I, Mr. Rickenbacker said, but I'll be

damned if I can jump like that. Let's say no more about it.

I flung off my shirt and stood stripped to the waist, a good deal of hair bristling on my chest.

You see? Miss Ogilvie said. A writer.

Inhale, Mr. Rickenbacker said.

For how long? I asked.

As long as possible, Mr. Rickenbacker said.

I began to inhale. Four minutes later I was still doing so. Naturally, the examining staff was a little amazed. They called a speedy meeting while I continued to inhale. After two minutes of heated debate the staff decided to ask me to stop inhaling. Miss Ogilvie explained that unless they did so I would be likely to go on inhaling all afternoon.

That will be enough for the present, Mr. Rickenbacker said.

Already? I'm not even started.

Now exhale.

For how long?

My God! Mr. Rickenbacker said.

You'd better tell him, Miss Ogilvie said. Otherwise he'll exhale all afternoon.

Three or four minutes, Mr. Rickenbacker said.

I exhaled for three minutes and was then asked to put on my shirt and go away.

How are things? I asked the staff. Am I in pretty good shape?

Let's say no more about it, Mr. Rickenbacker said. Please go away.

The following year our Board of Education decided to give no more physical examinations, which were all right as far as future captains of industry were concerned, and future statesmen, but only confusing when it came to future poets.

The
Fifty-Yard
Dash

After a certain letter came to me from New York the year I was twelve, I made up my mind to become the most powerful man in my neighborhood. The letter was from my friend Lionel Strongfort. I had clipped a coupon from *Argosy All-Story Magazine,* signed it, placed it in an envelope, and mailed it to him. He had written back promptly, with an enthusiasm bordering on pure delight, saying I was undoubtedly a man of uncommon intelligence, potentially a giant, and—unlike the average run-of-the-mill people of the world who were, in a manner of speaking, dreamwalkers and daydreamers—a person who would some day be somebody.

His opinion of me was very much like my own. It was pleasant, however, to have the opinion so emphatically corroborated, particularly by a man in New York—and a man with the greatest chest expansion in the world. With the letter came several photographic reproductions of Mr. Strongfort wearing nothing but a little bit of leopard skin. He was a tremendous man and claimed that at one time he had been puny. He was loaded all over with muscle and appeared to be somebody who could lift a 1920 Ford roadster and tip it over.

It was an honor to have him for a friend.

The only trouble was—I didn't have the money. I forget how much the exact figure was at the beginning of our acquaintanceship, but I haven't forgotten that it was an amount completely out of the question. While I was eager to be grateful to Mr. Strongfort for his enthusiasm, I didn't seem to be able to find words with which to explain about not having the money, without immediately appearing to be a dreamwalker and a daydreamer myself. So, while waiting from one day to another, looking everywhere for words that would not blight our friendship and degrade me to commonness, I talked the matter over with my uncle Gyko, who was studying Oriental philosophy at the time. He was amazed at my curious ambition, but quite pleased. He said the secret of greatness, according to Yoga, was the releasing within one's self of those mysterious vital forces which are in all men.

These strength, he said in English which he liked

to affect when speaking to me, ease from God. I tell you, Aram, eat ease wonderful.

I told him I couldn't begin to become the powerful man I had decided to become until I sent Mr. Strongfort some money.

Mohney! my uncle said with contempt. I tell you, Aram, mohney is nawthing. You cannot bribe God.

Although my uncle Gyko wasn't exactly a puny man, he was certainly not the man Lionel Strongfort was. In a wrestling match I felt certain Mr. Strongfort would get a headlock or a half-nelson or a toe-hold on my uncle and either make him give up or squeeze him to death. And then again, on the other hand, I wondered. My uncle was nowhere near as big as Mr. Strongfort, but neither was Mr. Strongfort as dynamically furious as my uncle. It seemed to me that, at best, Mr. Strongfort, in a match with my uncle, would have a great deal of unfamiliar trouble—I mean with the mysterious vital forces that were always getting released in my uncle, so that very often a swift glance from him would make a big man quail and turn away, or, if he had been speaking, stop quickly.

Long before I had discovered words with which to explain to Mr. Strongfort about the money, another letter came from him. It was as cordial as the first, and as a matter of fact, if anything, a little more cordial. I was delighted and ran about, releasing mysterious vital forces, turning handsprings, scrambling up trees, rolling somersaults, trying to tip over 1920 Ford roadsters, challenging all comers to wrestle, and in many other ways alarming my relatives and irritating the neighbors.

Not only was Mr. Strongfort not sore at me, he had reduced the cost of the course. Even so, the money necessary was still more than I could get hold of. I was selling papers every day, but *that* money was for bread and stuff like that. For a while I got up very early every morning and went around town looking for a small satchel full of money. During six days of this adventuring I found a nickel and two pennies. I found also a woman's purse containing several foul-smelling cosmetic items, no money, and a slip of paper on which was written in an ignorant hand: Steve Hertwig, 3764 Ventura Avenue.

Three days after the arrival of Mr. Strongfort's second letter, his third letter came. From this time on our correspondence became one-sided. In fact, I didn't write at all. Mr. Strongfort's communications were overpowering and not at all easy to answer, without money. There was, in fact, almost nothing to say.

It was wintertime when the first letter came, and it was then that I made up my mind to become the most powerful man in my neighborhood and ultimately, for all I knew, one of the most powerful men in the world. I had ideas of my own as to how to go about getting that way, but I had also the warm friendship and high regard of Mr. Strongfort in New York, and the mystical and furious guardianship of my uncle Gyko, at home.

The letters from Mr. Strongfort continued to arrive every two or three days all winter and on into springtime. I remember, the day apricots were ripe enough to steal, the arrival of a most charming letter from my friend in New York. It was a hymn to newness on earth, the arrival of springtime, the time of youth in the heart, of renewal, fresh strength, fresh determination, and many other things. It was truly a beautiful epistle, probably as fine as any to the Romans or anybody else. It was full of the legend-quality, the world-feeling, and the dignity-of-strength-feeling so characteristic of Biblical days. The last paragraph of the lovely hymn brought up, apologetically, the coarse theme of money. The sum was six or seven times as little as it had been originally, and a new element had come into Mr. Strongfort's program of changing me over from a nobody to a giant of tremendous strength, and extreme attractiveness to women. Mr. Strongfort had decided, he said, to teach me everything in one fell swoop, or one sweep fall, or something of that sort. At any rate, for three dollars, he said, he would send me all his precious secrets in one envelope and the rest would be up to me.

I took the matter up with my uncle Gyko, who by this time had reached the stage of fasting, meditating, walking for hours, and vibrating. We had had discussions two or three times a week all winter and he had told me in his own unique broken-English way all the secrets *he* had been learning from Yoga.

I tell you, Aram, I can do *anything*. Eat ease wonderful.

I believed him, too, even though he had lost a lot
of weight, couldn't sleep, and had a strange dy-
namic blaze in his eyes. He was very scornful of the
world that year and was full of pity for the dumb
beautiful animals that man was mistreating, killing,
eating, domesticating, and teaching to do tricks.

I tell you, Aram, eat ease creaminal to make the
horses work. To keal the cows. To teach the dogs to
jump, and the monkeys to smoke pipes.

I told him about the letter from Mr. Strongfort.

Mohney! he said. Always he wants mohney. I do
not like heem.

My uncle was getting all his dope free from the
theosophy-philosophy-astrology-and-miscellaneous
shelf at the Public Library. He believed, however,
that he was getting it straight from God. Before he
took up Yoga he had been one of the boys around
town and a good drinker of *rakhi,* but after the light
began to come to him he gave up drinking. He said
he was drinking liquor finer than *rakhi* or anything
else.

What's that? I asked him.

Aram, he said, eat ease weasdom.

Anyhow, he had little use for Mr. Strongfort and
regarded the man as a charlatan.

He's all right, I told him.

But my uncle became furious, releasing mysterious vital forces, and said, I wheel break hease head,
fooling all you leatle keads.

He ain't fooling, I said. He says he'll give me all his secrets for three dollars.

I tell you, Aram, he does not know any seacrets. He ease a liar.

I don't know about that. I'd like to try that stuff.

Eat ease creaminal, my uncle Gyko said, but I wheel geave you tree dollar.

He gave me the necessary three dollars and I sent them along to Mr. Strongfort. The envelope came from New York, full of Mr. Strongfort's secrets. They were strangely simple. It was all stuff I had known anyhow but had been too lazy to pay any attention to. The idea was to get up early in the morning and for an hour or so to do various kinds of acrobatic exercises, which were illustrated. Also to drink plenty of water, get plenty of fresh air, eat good wholesome food, and keep it up until you were a giant.

I felt a little let down and sent Mr. Strongfort a short polite note saying so. He ignored the note and I never heard from him again. In the meantime, I had been following the rules and growing more powerful every day. When I say *in the meantime*, I mean for four days I followed the rules. On the fifth day I decided to sleep instead of getting up and filling the house with noise and getting my grandmother sore. She used to wake up in the darkness of early morning and shout that I was an impractical fool and would never be rich. She would go back to sleep for five minutes, wake up, and then shout that I would never buy and sell for a profit. She would sleep a little more, waken, and shout that there were once three sons of a king; one was wise like his father; the other was crazy about girls; and the third had less brains than a bird. Then she would get out of bed, and, shouting steadily, tell me the whole story while I did my exercises.

The story would usually warn me to be sensible and not go around waking her up before daybreak all the time. That would always be the moral, more or less, although the story itself would be about three sons of some king, or three brothers, each of them very wealthy and usually very greedy, or three daughters, or three proverbs, or three roads, or something else like that.

She was wasting her breath, though, because I wasn't enjoying the early-morning acrobatics any more than she was. In fact, I was beginning to feel that it was a lot of nonsense, and that my uncle Gyko had been right about Mr. Strongfort in the first place.

So I gave up Mr. Strongfort's program and returned to my own, which was more or less as follows: to take it easy and grow to be the most powerful man in the neighborhood without any trouble or exercise. Which is what I did.

That spring Longfellow School announced that a track meet was to be held, one school to compete against another; *everybody* to participate.

Here, I believed, was my chance. In my opinion I would be first in every event.

Somehow or other, however, continuous meditation on the theme of athletics had the effect of growing into a fury of anticipation that continued all day and all night, so that before the day of the track meet I had run the fifty-yard dash any number of hundreds of times, had jumped the running broad jump, the standing broad jump, and the high jump, and in each event had made my competitors look like weaklings.

This tremendous inner activity, which was strictly Yoga, changed on the day of the track meet into fever.

The time came at last for me and three other athletes, one of them a Greek, to go to our marks, get set, and go; and I did, in a blind rush of speed which I knew had never before occurred in the history of athletics.

It seemed to me that never before had any living man moved so swiftly. Within myself I ran the fifty yards fifty times before I so much as opened my eyes to find out how far back I had left the other runners. I was very much amazed at what I saw.

Three boys were four yards ahead of me and going away.

It was incredible. It was unbelievable, but it was obviously the truth. There ought to be some mistake, but there wasn't. There they were, ahead of me, going away.

Well, it simply meant that I would have to overtake them, with my eyes open, and win the race. This I proceeded to do. They continued, incredibly, however, to go away, in spite of my intention. I became irritated and decided to put them in their places for the impertinence, and began releasing all the mysterious vital forces within myself that I had. Somehow or other, however, not even this seemed to bring me any closer to them and I felt that in some strange way I was being betrayed. If so, I decided, I would shame my betrayer by winning the race in spite of the betrayal, and once again I threw fresh life and energy into my running. There wasn't a great distance still to go, but I knew I would be able to do it.

Then I knew I wouldn't.

The race was over.

I was last, by ten yards.

Without the slightest hesitation I protested and challenged the runners to another race, same distance, back. They refused to consider the proposal, which proved, I knew, that they were afraid to race me. I told them they knew very well I could beat them.

It was very much the same in all the other events.

When I got home I was in high fever and very angry. I was delirious all night and sick three days. My grandmother took very good care of me and probably was responsible for my not dying. When my uncle Gyko came to visit me he was no longer hollow-cheeked. It seems he had finished his fast, which had been a long one—forty days or so; and nights too, I believe. He had stopped meditating, too, because he had practically exhausted the subject. He was again one of the boys around town, drinking, staying up all hours, and following the women.

I tell you, Aram, he said, we are a great family. We can do *anything*.

A Nice Old-Fashioned Romance, with Love Lyrics and Everything

My cousin Arak was a year and a half younger than me, round-faced, dark, and exceptionally elegant in manners. It was no pretense with him. His manners were just naturally that way, just as my manners were bad from the beginning. Where Arak would get around any sort of complication at school with a bland smile that showed his front upper teeth, separated, and melted the heart of stone of our teacher, Miss Daffney, I would go to the core of the complication and with noise and vigor prove that Miss Daffney or somebody else was the culprit, not me, and if need be, I would carry the case to the Supreme Court and prove my innocence.

I usually got sent to the office. In some cases I would get a strapping for debating the case in the office against Mr. Derringer, our principal, who was no earthly good at debates. The minute I got him cornered he got out his strap.

Arak was different; he didn't care to fight for justice. He wasn't anywhere near as bright as me, but even though he was a year and a half younger than me, he was in the same grade. I usually won all my arguments with my teachers, but instead of being glad to get rid of me they refused to promote me, in the hope, I believe, of winning the following semester's arguments and getting even. That's how it happened that I came to be the oldest pupil in the fifth grade.

One day Miss Daffney tried to tell the world I was the author of the poem on the blackboard that said she was in love with Mr. Derringer, and ugly. The author of the poem was my cousin Arak, not me. Any poem I wrote wouldn't be about Miss Daffney, it would be about something worthwhile. Nevertheless, without mentioning any names, but with a ruler in her hand, Miss Daffney stood beside my desk and said, I am going to find out who is responsible for this horrible outrage on the blackboard and see that he is properly punished.

He? I said. How do you know it's a boy and not a girl?

Miss Daffney whacked me on the knuckles of my right hand. I jumped out of my seat and said, You can't go around whacking me on the knuckles. I'll report this.

Sit down, Miss Daffney said.

I did. She had me by the right ear, which was getting out of shape from being grabbed hold of by Miss Daffney and other teachers.

I sat down and quietly, almost inaudibly, said, You'll hear about this.

Hold your tongue, Miss Daffney said, and although I was outraged by what was happening, I stuck out my tongue and held it, while the little Mexican, Japanese, Armenian, Greek, Italian, Portuguese, and plain American boys and girls in the class, who looked to me for comedy, roared with laughter. Miss Daffney came down on my hand with the ruler, but this time the ruler grazed my nose. This to me was particularly insulting, inasmuch as my nose then, as now, was large. A small nose would not have been grazed, and I took Miss Daffney's whack as a subtle comment on the size of my nose.

I put my bruised hand over my hurt nose and again rose to my feet.

You told me to hold my tongue, I said, insisting that I had done no evil, had merely carried out her instructions, and was therefore innocent, utterly undeserving of the whacked hand and the grazed nose.

You be good now, Miss Daffney said. I won't stand any more of your nonsense. You be good.

I took my hand away from my nose and began to be good. I smiled like a boy bringing her a red apple. My audience roared with laughter and Miss Daffney dropped the ruler, reached for me, fell over the desk, got up, and began to chase me around the room.

There I go again, I kept saying to myself while Miss Daffney chased me around the room. There I go again getting in a mess like this that's sure to end in murder, while my cousin Arak, who is the guilty one, sits there and smiles. There's no justice anywhere.

When Miss Daffney finally caught me, as I knew she would unless I wanted even more severe punishment from Mr. Derringer, there was a sort of free-for-all during which she tried to gouge my eyes out, pull off my ears, fingers, and arms, and I, by argument, tried to keep her sweet and ladylike.

When she was exhausted, I went back to my seat, and the original crime of the day was taken up again: Who was the author of the love lyric on the blackboard?

Miss Daffney straightened her hair and her clothes, got her breath, demanded and got silence, and after several moments of peace during which the ticking of the clock was heard, she began to speak.

I am going to ask each of you by name if you wrote this awful—poem—on the blackboard and I shall expect you to tell the truth. If you lie, I shall find out anyway and your punishment will be all the worse.

She began to ask the boys and girls if they had written the poem and of course they hadn't. Then she asked my cousin Arak and he also said he hadn't. Then she asked me and I said I hadn't, which was the truth.

You go to the office, she said. You liar.

I didn't write any poem on any blackboard, I said. And I'm not a liar.

Mr. Derringer received me with no delight. Two minutes later, Susie Kokomoto arrived from our class with a message describing my crime. In fact, quoting it. Mr. Derringer read the message, made six or seven faces, smiled, snapped his suspenders, coughed and said, What made you write this little poem?

I didn't write it.

Naturally, you'd *say* you didn't, but why did you?

I *didn't* write it.

Now don't be headstrong, Mr. Derringer said. That's a rather alarming rumor to be spreading. How do you *know* Miss Daffney's in love with me? *Is she?*

Well, that's what it says here. What gave you that impression? Have you noticed her looking at me with admiration or something?

I haven't noticed her looking at you with anything. Are *you* in love with *her* or something?

That remains to be seen, Mr. Derringer said. It isn't a bad poem, up to a point. Do you really regard Miss Daffney as ugly?

I didn't write the poem. I can prove it. I don't write that way.

You mean your handwriting isn't like the handwriting on the blackboard?

Yes, and I don't write that kind of poetry either.

You *admit* writing poetry? Mr. Derringer said.

I write poetry, but not *that* kind of poetry.

A rumor like that. I hope you know what you're about.

Well, all I know is I didn't write it.

Personally, Mr. Derringer said, I think Miss Daffney is not only not ugly, but on the contrary attractive.

Well, that's all right. The only thing I want is not to get into a lot of trouble over something I didn't do.

You *could* have written the poem, Mr. Derringer said.

Not *that* one. I could have written a good one.

What do you mean, *good?* Beautiful? Or insulting?

I mean beautiful, only it wouldn't be about Miss Daffney.

Up to this point, Mr. Derringer said, I was willing to entertain doubts as to your being the author of the poem, but no longer. I am convinced you wrote it. Therefore I must punish you.

I got up and started to debate.

You give me a strapping for something I didn't do, and you'll hear about it.

So he gave me a strapping and *the whole school* heard about it. I went back to class limping. The poem had been erased. All was well again. The culprit had been duly punished, the poem effaced, and order re-established in the fifth grade. My cousin Arak sat quietly admiring Alice Bovard's brown curls.

First thing during recess I knocked him down and sat on him.

I got a strapping for that, I said, so don't write any more of them.

The next morning, however, there was another love lyric on the blackboard in my cousin Arak's unmistakable hand, and in his unmistakable style, and once again Miss Daffney wanted to weed out the culprit and have him punished. When I came into the room and saw the poem and the lay of the land I immediately began to object. My cousin Arak was going too far. In Armenian I began to swear at him. He, however, had become stone deaf, and Miss Daffney believed my talk was for her. Here, here, she said. Speak in a language everybody can understand if you've got something to say.

All I've got to say is I didn't write that poem. And I didn't write yesterday's, either. If I get into any more trouble on account of these poems, somebody's going to hear about it.

Sit down, Miss Daffney said.

After the roll call, Miss Daffney filled a whole sheet of paper with writing, including the new poem, and ordered me to take the message to the office.

Why *me?* I didn't write the poem.

Do as you're told.

I went to her desk, put out my hand to take the note, Miss Daffney gave it a whack with a ruler, I jumped back three feet and shouted, I'm not going to carry love-letters for you.

This just naturally was the limit. There was a limit to everything. Miss Daffney leaped at me. I in turn was so sore at my cousin Arak that I turned around and jumped on him. He pretended to be very innocent, and offered no resistance. He was very deft, though, and instead of getting the worst of it, he got the least, while I fell all over the floor until Miss Daffney caught up with me. After that it was all her fight. When I got to the office with the message, I had scratches and bruises all over my face and hands, and the love-letter from Miss Daffney to Mr. Derringer was crumbled and in places torn.

What's been keeping you? Mr. Derringer said. Here, let me see that message. What mischief have you been up to now?

He took the message, unfolded it, smoothed it out on his desk, and read it very slowly. He read it three or four times. He was delighted, and, as far as. I could tell, in love. He turned with a huge smile on his face and was about to reprimand me again for saying that Miss Daffney was ugly.

I didn't write the poem, I said. I didn't write yesterday's either. All I want is a chance to get myself a little education and live and let live.

Now, now, Mr. Derringer said.

He was quite pleased.

If you're in love with her, I said, that's your affair, but leave me out of it.

All I say is you could be a little more gracious about Miss Daffney's appearance, Mr. Derringer said. If she seems plain to you, perhaps she doesn't seem plain to someone else.

I was disgusted. It was just no use.

All right, I said. Tomorrow I'll be gracious.

Now that's better, Mr. Derringer said. Of course I must punish you.

He reached for the lower drawer of his desk where the strap was.

Oh, no, I said. If you punish me, then I won't be gracious.

Well, what about today's poem? I've got to punish you for that. Tomorrow's will be another story.

No sir. Nothing doing.

Oh, all right, Mr. Derringer said, but see that you're gracious.

Can I go back now?

Yes, I think so.

I began to leave the office.

Wait a minute, he said. Everybody'll know something fishy's going on somewhere unless they hear you howl. Better howl ten times, and then go back.

Howl? I can't howl unless I'm hurt.

Of course you can, Mr. Derringer said. Just give out a big painful howl. You can do it.

I don't think I can.

I'll hit this chair ten times with the strap, and you howl.

Mr. Derringer hit the chair with the strap and I tried to howl the way I had howled yesterday, but it didn't sound real. It sounded fishy, somewhere.

We were going along that way when Miss Daffney herself came into the office, only we didn't know she'd come in, on account of the noise.

On the tenth one I turned to Mr. Derringer and said, That's ten.

Then, I saw Miss Daffney. She was aghast and mouth-agape.

Just a few more, son, Mr. Derringer said, for good measure.

Before I could tell him Miss Daffney was in the office, he was whacking the chair again and I was howling.

It was crazy.

Miss Daffney coughed and Mr. Derringer turned and saw her—his beloved.

Miss Daffney didn't speak. She *couldn't*. Mr. Derringer smiled. He was very embarrassed and began swinging the strap around.

I'll not have any pupil of this school being impertinent, Mr. Derringer said.

He was madly in love with her and was swinging the strap around and trying to put over a little personality. Miss Daffney, however, just didn't think very much of his punishing the boy by hitting a chair, while the boy howled, the man and the boy together making a mockery of justice and true love. She gave him a very dirty look.

Oh! Mr. Derringer said. You mean about my hitting the chair? We were just rehearsing, weren't we, son?

No, we weren't, I said.

Miss Daffney, infuriated, turned and fled, and Mr. Derringer sat down.

Now look what you've done, he said.

Well, I said, if you're going to have a romance with her, have it, but don't mess me up in it.

Well, Mr. Derringer said, I guess that's that.

He was a very sad man.

All right, he said, go back to your class.

I want you to know I didn't write those poems.

That's got nothing to do with it.

I thought you might want to know.

It's too late now. She'll never admire me any more.

Why don't you write a poem to her yourself?

I can't write poems, Mr. Derringer said.

Well, figure it out some way.

When I went back to class Miss Daffney was very polite. So was I. She knew I knew and she knew if she got funny I'd either ruin the romance or make her marry him, so she was very friendly. In two weeks school closed and when school opened again Miss Daffney didn't show up. Either Mr. Derringer didn't write her a poem, or did and it was no good; or he didn't tell her he loved her, or did and she didn't care; or else he proposed to her and she turned him down, *because I knew*, and got herself transferred to another school so she could get over her broken heart.

Something like that.

My Cousin Dikran, the Orator

Twenty years ago, in the San Joaquin Valley, the Armenians used to regard oratory as the greatest, the noblest, the most important, one might say the *only*, art. About ninety-two per cent of the vineyardists around Fresno, by actual count, believed that any man who could make a speech was a cultured man. This was so, I imagine after all these years, because the vineyardists themselves were so ineffective at speechmaking, so self-conscious about it, so embarrassed, and so profoundly impressed by public speakers who could get up on a platform, adjust spectacles on their noses, look at their pocket watches, cough politely, and, beginning quietly, lift their voices to a roar that shook the farmers to the roots and made them know the speaker was educated.

What language! What energy! What wisdom! What magnificent roaring! the farmers said to themselves.

The farmers, assembled in the basement of one or another of the three churches, or in the Civic Auditorium, trembled with awe, wiped the tears from their eyes, blew their noses, and, momentarily overcome, donated as much money as they could afford. On some occasions, such as when money was being raised for some especially intimate cause, the farmers, in donating money, would stand up in the auditorium and cry out, Mgerdich Kasabian, his wife Araxie, his three sons, Gourken, Sirak, and Toumas —fifty cents! and sit down amid thunderous applause, not so much for the sum of money donated as for the magnificent manner of speaking, and the excellent and dramatic pronunciation of the fine old-country names: Mgerdich, Araxie, Gourken, Sirak, Toumas.

In this matter of speaking and donating money, the farmers competed with one another. If a farmer did not get up and publicly make his announcement like a man—well, then, the poor fellow! Neither money nor the heart to get up fearlessly and throw away the trembling in his soul! Because of this competition, a farmer unable to donate money (but with every impulse in the world to help the cause), would sit nervously in shame year after year, and then finally, with the arrival of better days, leap to his feet, look about the auditorium furiously, and shout, Gone are the days of poverty for this tribe from the lovely city of Dikranagert—the five Pampalonian brothers—twenty-five cents! and go home with his head high, and his heart higher. Poor? In the old days, yes. But no more. (And the five enormous men would look at one another with family pride, and push their sons before them—with affection, of course; that strange Near-Eastern, Oriental affection that came from delight in no longer being humiliated in the eyes of one's countrymen.)

No farmer was prouder, however, than when his son, at school, at church, at a picnic, or anywhere, got up and made a speech.

The boy! the farmer would shout at his eighty-eight-year-old father. Listen to him! It's Vahan, my son, *your* grandson—eleven years old. He's talking about Europe.

The grandfather would shake his head and wonder what it was all about, a boy of eleven so serious and so well-informed, talking about Europe. The old man would scarcely know where Europe was, although he would know he had visited Havre, in France, on his way to America. Perhaps Havre—perhaps that was it. *Yevroba.* Europe. But what in the world could be the matter with Havre suddenly

—to make the boy so tense and excited? Ahkh, the old man would groan, it is all beyond me. I don't remember. It was a pleasant city on the sea, with ships.

The women would be overjoyed and full of amazement at themselves, the mothers. They would look about at one another, nodding, shaking their heads, and after ten minutes of the boy's talking in English, which they couldn't understand, they would burst into sweet silent tears because it was all so amazing and wonderful—little Berjie, only yesterday a baby who couldn't speak two words of Armenian, let alone English, on a platform, speaking, swinging his arms, pointing a finger, now at the ceiling, now west, now south, now north, and occasionally at his heart.

It was inevitable under these circumstances for the Garoghlanians to produce an orator too, even though the Old Man regarded speechmakers as fools and frauds.

When you hear a small man with spectacles on his face shouting from the bottom of his bowels, let me tell you that that man is either a jackass or a liar.

He was always impatient with any kind of talk, except the most direct and pertinent. He wanted to know what he didn't know, and that was all. He wanted no talk for talk's sake. He used to go to all the public meetings, but they never failed to sicken him. Every speaker would watch his face to learn how displeased the Old Man was, and when they saw his lips moving with silent curses they would calm down and try to talk sense, or, if they had talked to him in private and learned how stupid he regarded them, they would try to get even with him by shouting louder than ever and occasionally coming forth with, We know there are those among us who scoff at us, who ridicule our efforts, who even, out of fantastic pride of heart, regard us as fools, but this has always been the cross we have had to carry, and carry it we will.

Here the Old Man would tap his sons on their heads, these in turn would tap their sons on their heads, these would nudge one another, the women would look about, and together the Garoghlanians, numbering thirty-seven or thirty-eight, would rise and walk out, with the Old Man looking about furiously at the poor farmers and saying, They're carrying the cross again—let's go.

In spite of all this, I say, it was inevitable for the Garoghlanians to produce an orator. It was the style, the will of the people, and some member of the Garoghlanian tribe would naturally find it essential to enter the field and show everybody what oratory could really be—what, in fact, it really was, if the truth were known.

This Garoghlanian turned out to be my little cousin Dikran, my uncle Zorab's second son, who was nine years old when the war ended, a year younger than myself, but so much smaller in size that I regarded him as somebody to ignore.

From the beginning this boy was one of those

very bright boys who have precious little real understanding, no humor at all, and the disgraceful and insulting attitude that all knowledge comes from the outside—disgraceful particularly to the Garoghlanians, who for centuries had come by all their wisdom naturally, from within. It was the boast of the Old Man that any real Garoghlanian could spot a crook in one glance, and would have the instinctive good sense to know how to deal with the man.

When you look at a man who hides behind his face, the Old Man used to say, let me tell you that that man is no good. He is either a spy or a swindler. On the other hand, if you look at a man whose glance tells you, *Brother, I am your brother*—watch out. That man carries a knife on his person somewhere.

With instruction of this sort, beginning practically at birth, it was only natural for the average Garoghlanian to grow up in wisdom of the world and its strange inhabitants.

The only Garoghlanian who couldn't catch on, however, was this cousin of mine, Dikran. He was strictly a book-reader, a type of human being extremely contemptible to the Old Man, unless he could perceive definite improvement in the character of the reader—of necessity a child, as who else would read a book? In the case of Dikran, the Old Man could perceive no improvement; on the contrary, a continuous decline in understanding, until at last, when the boy was eleven, the Old Man was

informed that Dikran was the brightest pupil at
Longfellow School, the pride of his teachers and an
accomplished public speaker.

When this news was brought to the Old Man by
the boy's mother, the Old Man, who was lying on
the couch in the parlor, turned his face to the wall
and groaned, Too bad. What a waste. What's eating
the boy?

Why, he's the brightest boy in the whole school,
the mother said.

The Old Man sat up and said, When you hear of a
boy of eleven being the brightest boy in a school of
five hundred boys—pay no attention to it. For the
love of God, what's he bright *about?* Isn't he eleven?
What bright? Who wants a child to burden himself
with such a pathetic sense of importance? You have
been a poor mother, I must tell you. Drive the poor
boy out of the house into the fields. Let him go
swimming with his cousins. The poor fellow doesn't
even know how to laugh. And you come here in
the afternoon to tell me he is bright. Well, go away.

In spite of even this, I say, the boy moved steadily
forward, turning the pages of books day and night,
Sundays and holidays and picnic days, until finally,
on top of everything else, it was necessary to fit
glasses to his face—which made him all the more
miserable-looking, so that every time there was a
family gathering the Old Man would look about,
see the boy, and groan, My God, the philosopher!
All right, boy, come here.

The boy would get up and stand in front of the Old Man.

Well, the Old Man would say, you read books. That's fine. You are now eleven years old. Thank God for that. Now tell me—what do you know? What have you learned?

I can't tell you in Armenian, the boy would say.

I see, the Old Man would say. Well, tell me in English.

Here everything would go haywire. This little cousin of mine, eleven years old, would really begin to make a speech about all the wonderful things he had found out from the books. They *were* wonderful, too. He knew all the dates, all the reasons, all the names, all the places, and what the consequences were likely to be.

It was very beautiful in a minor, melancholy way.

Suddenly the Old Man would stop the boy's speech, shouting, What are you—a parrot?

Even so, it seemed to me that the Old Man was fond of this strange arrival among the Garoghlanians. Book-readers were fools—and so were orators —but at any rate *our* book-reader and orator was not by any means a run-of-the-mill book-reader and orator. He was at any rate something special. For one thing he was younger than the others who imagined they had learned many things from books, and for another he spoke a lot more clearly than the others.

For these reasons, and because of the evident determination in the boy to follow his own inclination, he was accepted by all of us as the Garoghlanian scholar and orator, and permitted to occupy his time and develop whatever mind he may have been born with as he pleased.

In 1920, Longfellow School announced an evening program consisting of (1) Glee Club Singing, (2) a performance of *Julius Caesar*, and (3) a speech by Dikran Garoghlanian—a speech entitled *Was the World War Fought in Vain?* At the proper time the Garoghlanians seated themselves in the school auditorium, listened to the awful singing, watched the horrible performance of *Julius Caesar*, and then listened to the one and only Garoghlanian orator—Dikran, the second son of Zorab.

The speech was flawless: dramatic, well-uttered, intelligent, and terribly convincing—the conclusion being that the World War had *not* been fought in vain, that Democracy *had* saved the world. Everybody in the auditorium was stricken with awe, and applauded the speech wildly. It was really too much, though—I mean for the Old Man. In the midst of the thunderous applause, he burst out laughing. The speech was really splendid, in a way. It was at least the best thing of its kind—the best of the worst kind of thing. There was some occasion for pride in this, even.

That evening at home the Old Man called the boy to him and said, I listened to your speech. It's all right. I understand you spoke about a war in which several million men were killed. I understand you *proved* the war was not fought in vain. I must tell you I am rather pleased. A statement as large and as beautiful as that deserves to come only from the lips of a boy of eleven—from one who believes what he is saying. From a grown man, I must tell you, the horror of that remark would be just a little too much for me to endure. Continue your investigation of the world from books, and I am sure, if you are diligent and your eyes hold out, that by the time you are sixty-seven you will know the awful foolishness of that remark—so innocently uttered by yourself tonight, in such a pure flow of soprano English. In a way I am as proud of you as of any other member of this tribe. You may all go now. I want to sleep. I am not eleven years old. I am sixty-seven.

Everybody got up and went away, except me. I stayed behind long enough to see the old man take off his shoes and hear him sigh, These crazy miraculous children of this crazy miraculous family.

The Presbyterian Choir Singers

One of the many curious and delightful things about our country is the ease with which our good people move from one religion to another, or from no particular religion at all to any religion that happens to come along, without experiencing any particular loss or gain, and go right on being innocent anyhow.

Myself, I was born, for instance, a kind of Catholic, although I was not baptized until I was thirteen, a circumstance which, I remember clearly, irritated the priest and impelled him to ask my people if they were crazy, to which my people replied, We have been away.

Thirteen years old and not baptized! the priest shouted. What kind of people are you?

For the most part, my uncle Melik replied, we are an agricultural people, although we have had our brilliant men, too.

It was a Saturday afternoon. The whole thing took no more than seven minutes, but even after I was baptized it was impossible for me to feel any change.

Well, my grandmother said, you are now baptized. Do you feel any better?

For some months, I believe I ought to explain, I had been feeling intelligent, which led my grandmother to suspect that I was ill with some mysterious illness or that I was losing my mind.

I think I feel the same, I said.

Do you believe now? she shouted. Or do you still have doubts?

I can easily *say* I believe, but to tell you the truth I don't know for sure. I want to be a Christian of course.

Well, just believe then, and go about your business.

My business was in some ways ordinary and in other ways incredible.

I sang in the Boys' Choir at the Presbyterian Church on Tulare Street. For doing so I received one dollar a week from an elderly Christian lady named Balaifal who lived in sorrow and solitude in the small ivy-covered house next to the house in which my friend Pandro Kolkhozian lived.

This boy, like myself, was loud in speech. That is to say, we swore a good deal—in all innocence of course—and by doing so grieved Miss or Mrs. Balaifal so much that she sought to save us while there was still time. To be saved was a thing I for one had no occasion to resist or resent.

Miss Balaifal (I shall call her that from now on, since while I knew her she was certainly single, and since I do not know for sure if she ever married, or for that matter if she ever thought of marrying, or if she ever so much as fell in love—earlier in life of course, and no doubt with a scoundrel who took the whole matter with a grain of salt)—Miss Balaifal, as I began to say, was a cultured woman, a reader of the poems of Robert Browning and a woman of great sensitivity, so that coming out on the porch of her house to hear us talk she could stand so much and no more, and when the limit had been reached, cried out, Boys, boys. You must not use profane language.

Pandro Kolkhozian, on the one hand, *seemed* to be the most uncouth boy in the world and on the other —and this was the quality in him which endeared him to me—was *actually* the most courteous and thoughtful.

Yes, Miss Balaifum, he said.

Balaifal, the lady corrected him. Please come here. Both of you.

We went to Miss Balaifal and asked what she wanted.

What do you want, Miss Balaifum? Pandro said.

Miss Balaifal went into her coat pocket and brought out a sheaf of pamphlets, and without looking at them handed one to each of us. My pamphlet was entitled *Redemption, The Story of a Drunkard.* Pandro's was entitled *Peace at Last, The Story of a Drunkard.*

What's this for? Pandro said.

I want you boys to read those pamphlets and try to be good. I want you to stop using profane language.

It doesn't say anything here about profane language, Pandro said.

There's a good lesson for each of you in those pamphlets. Read them and don't use profane language any more.

Yes, ma'am, I said. Is that all?

One thing more. I wonder if you boys would help me move the organ from the dining room to the parlor?

Sure, Miss Balaifum, Pandro said. Any time.

So we went into the lady's house and, while she instructed us in just how to do it without damaging the instrument or ourselves, we moved it, by slow degrees, from the dining room to the parlor.

Now read those pamphlets, Miss Balaifal said.

Yes, ma'am, Pandro said. Is that all?

Well, now, the lady said. I want you to sing while I play the organ.

I can't sing, Miss Balaifum.

Nonsense. Of course you can sing, Pedro.

Pandro. Pedro is my cousin's name.

As a matter of fact Pandro's name was Panvor, which in Armenian means prisoner. When he had started to school his teacher hadn't cared for, or hadn't liked the sound of, Panvor, so she had written down on his card Pandro. As for his cousin's name, it was Bedros, with the *b* soft, which in turn had been changed at school to Pedro. It was all quite all right of course, and no harm to anybody.

Without answering him, the elderly lady sat on the stool, adjusted her feet on the pedals of the organ, and without any instructions to us, began to play a song which, from its dullness, was obviously religious. After a moment she herself began to sing. Pandro, in a soft voice, uttered a very profane, if not vulgar, word, which fortunately Miss Balaifal did not hear. Miss Balaifal's voice was, if anything, not impressive. The pedals squeaked a good deal louder than she sang, the tones of the organ were not any too clear, but even so, it was possible to know that Miss Balaifal's voice was not delightful.

Galilee, bright Galilee, she sang.

She turned to us, nodded, and said, Now sing, boys, sing.

We knew neither the words nor the music, but it seemed that common courtesy demanded at least an honest effort, which we made, trying as far as possible to follow the music coming out of the organ and the dramatic words coming out of Miss Balaifal.

Ruler of the storm was He, on the raging Galilee, she sang.

In all, we tried to sing three songs. After each song, Pandro would say, Thank you very much, Miss Balaifum. Can we go now?

At last she got up from the organ and said, I'm sure you're the better for it. If evil friends invite you to drink, turn away.

We'll turn away, Miss Balaifum, Pandro said. Won't we, Aram?

I will, I said.

I will too, Pandro said. Can we go now, Miss Balaifum?

Read the pamphlets, she said. It's not too late.

We'll read them, Pandro said. Just as soon as we get time.

We left the lady's house and went back to the front yard of Pandro's house and began to read the pamphlets. Before we were half through reading, the lady came out on the porch and in a very high and excited voice said, Which of you was it?

Which of us was *what?* Pandro said.

He was very bewildered.

Which of you was it that *sang?* Miss Balaifal said.

We both sang, I said.

No, Miss Balaifal said. Only one of you sang. One of you has a beautiful Christian voice.

Not me, Pandro said.

You, Miss Balaifal said to me. Eugene. Was it you?

Aram, I said. Not Eugene. No, I don't think it was me either.

Boys, come here, Miss Balaifal said.

Who? Pandro said.

Both of you, the lady said.

When we were in the house and Miss Balaifal was seated at the organ again Pandro said, I don't want to sing. I don't like to sing.

You sing, the lady said to me.

I sang.

Miss Balaifal leaped to her feet.

You are the one, she said. You must sing at church.

I won't.

You mustn't use profane language.

I'm not using profane language, and I promise not to use profane language again as long as I live, but I won't sing in church.

Your voice is the most Christian voice I have ever heard.

It isn't.

Yes, it is.

Well, I won't sing anyway.

You must, you must.

Thanks very much, Miss Balaifum, Pandro said. Can we go now? He doesn't want to sing in church.

He must, he must.

Why?

For the good of his soul.

Pandro whispered the profane word again.

Now tell me, the lady said. What is your name?
I told her.
You are a Christian of course?
I guess so.
A Presbyterian of course?
I don't know about that.
You are. Of course you are. I want you to sing in the Tulare Street Presbyterian Church—in the Boys' Choir—next Sunday.
Why? Pandro said again.
We need voices. We must have young voices. We must have singers. He must sing next Sunday.
I don't like to sing. I don't like to go to church either.
Boys, Miss Balaifal said. Sit down. I want to talk to you.
We sat down. Miss Balaifal talked to us for at least thirty minutes.
We didn't believe a word of it, although out of courtesy we kept answering her questions the way we knew she wanted us to answer them, but when she asked us to get down on our knees with her while she prayed, we wouldn't do it. Miss Balaifal argued this point for some time and then decided to let us have our way—for a moment. Then she tried again, but we still wouldn't do it. Pandro said we'd move the organ any time, or anything else like that, but we wouldn't get down on our knees.
Well, Miss Balaifal said, will you close your eyes?
What for? Pandro said.

It's customary for everybody to close his eyes while someone is praying.

Who's praying?

No one, *yet*. But if you'll promise to close your eyes, *I'll* pray, but you've got to promise to close your eyes.

What do you want to pray for?

I want to pray for you boys.

What for?

A little prayer for you won't do any harm, Miss Balaifal said. Will you close your eyes?

Oh! all right, Pandro said.

We closed our eyes and Miss Balaifal prayed.

It wasn't a little prayer by a long shot.

Amen, she said at last. Now, boys, don't you feel better?

In all truth, we didn't.

Yes, we do, Pandro said. Can we go now, Miss Balaifum? Any time you want the organ moved, we'll move it for you.

Sing for all you're worth, Miss Balaifal said to me, and turn away from any evil companion who invites you to drink.

Yes, ma'am.

You know where the church is?

What church?

The Tulare Street Presbyterian Church.

I know where it is.

Mr. Saugus will be expecting you Sunday morning at nine-thirty.

Well, it just seemed like I was cornered.

Pandro went with me to the church on Sunday, but refused to stand with the choir boys and sing. He sat in the last row of the church and watched and listened. As for myself, I was never more unhappy in my life, although I sang.

Never again, I told Pandro after it was all over.

The following Sunday I didn't show up of course, but that didn't do any good, because Miss Balaifal got us into her house again, played the organ, sang, made us try to sing, prayed, and was unmistakably determined to keep me in the Boys' Choir. I refused flatly, and Miss Balaifal decided to put the whole thing on a more worldly basis.

You have a rare Christian voice, she said. A voice needed by religion. You yourself are deeply religious, although you do not know it yet. Since this is so, let me ask you to sing for *me* every Sunday. I will *pay* you.

How much? Pandro said.

Fifty cents, Miss Balaifal said.

We usually sang four or five songs. It took about half an hour altogether, although we had to sit another hour while the preacher delivered his sermon. In short, it wasn't worth it.

For this reason I could make no reply.

Seventy-five cents, Miss Balaifal suggested.

The air was stuffy, the preacher was a bore, it was all very depressing.

One dollar, Miss Balaifal said. Not a cent more.

Make it a dollar and a quarter, Pandro said.

Not a cent more than a dollar, Miss Balaifal said.

He's got the best voice in the whole choir, Pandro said. *One* dollar? A voice like that is worth *two* dollars to any religion.

I've made my offer, Miss Balaifal said.

There are other religions, Pandro said.

This, I must say, upset Miss Balaifal.

His voice, she said bitterly, is a Christian voice, and what's more it's Presbyterian.

The Baptists would be glad to get a voice like that for two dollars, Pandro said.

The Baptists! Miss Balaifal said with some—I hesitate to say it—contempt.

They're no different than the Presbyterians, Pandro said.

One dollar, Miss Balaifal said. One dollar, and your name on the program.

I don't like to sing, Miss Balaifal, I said.

Yes, you do. You just think you don't. If you could see your face when you sing—why—

He's got a voice like an angel, Pandro said.

I'll fix you, I told Pandro in Armenian.

That's no one-dollar voice, Pandro said.

All right, boys, Miss Balaifal said. A dollar and fifteen cents, but no more.

A dollar and a quarter, Pandro said, or we go to the Baptists.

All right, Miss Balaifal said, but I must say you drive a hard bargain.

Wait a minute, I said. I don't like to sing. I won't sing for a dollar and a quarter or anything else.

A bargain is a bargain, Miss Balaifal said.

I didn't make any bargain. Pandro did. Let *him* sing.

He *can't* sing, Miss Balaifal said.

I've got the worst voice in the world, Pandro said with great pride.

His poor voice wouldn't be worth ten cents to anybody, Miss Balaifal said.

Not even a nickel, Pandro said.

Well, I'm not going to sing—for a dollar and a quarter or anything else. I don't need any money.

You made a bargain, Miss Balaifal said.

Yes, you did, Pandro said.

I jumped on Pandro right in Miss Balaifal's parlor and we began to wrestle. The elderly Christian lady tried to break it up, but since it was impossible to determine which of us was the boy with the angelic voice, she began to pray. The wrestling continued until most of the furniture in the room had been knocked over, except the organ. The match was finally a draw, the wrestlers exhausted and flat on their backs.

Miss Balaifal stopped praying and said, Sunday then, at a dollar and a quarter.

It took me some time to get my breath.

Miss Balaifal, I'll sing in that choir only if Pandro sings too.

But his voice is terrible.

I don't care what it is. If I sing, he's got to sing too.

I'm afraid he'd ruin the choir.

He's got to go up there with me every Sunday, or nothing doing.

Well, now, let me see, Miss Balaifal said.

She gave the matter considerable thought.

Suppose he goes up and stands in the choir, Miss Balaifal said, but *doesn't* sing? Suppose he just *pretends* to sing?

That's all right with me, but he's got to be there all the time.

What do *I* get? Pandro said.

Well, now, Miss Balaifal said, I surely can't be expected to pay you, too.

If I go up there, Pandro said, I've got to be paid.

All right, Miss Balaifal said. One dollar for the boy who sings; twenty-five cents for the boy who doesn't.

I've got the worst voice in the world, Pandro said.

You must be fair, Miss Balaifal said. After all, you won't be singing. You'll just be standing there with the other boys.

Twenty-five cents isn't enough.

We got off the floor and began rearranging the furniture.

All right, Miss Balaifal said. One dollar for the boy who sings. Thirty-five cents for the boy who doesn't.

Make it fifty, Pandro said.

Very well, then. A dollar for *you*. Fifty cents for *you*.

We start working next Sunday? Pandro said.

That's right, Miss Balaifal said. I'll pay you here after the services. Not a word of this to any of the other boys in the choir.

We won't mention it to anybody, Pandro said.

In this manner, in the eleventh year of my life, I became, more or less, a Presbyterian—at least every Sunday morning. It wasn't the money. It was simply that a bargain had been made, and that Miss Balaifal had her heart set on having me sing for religion.

As I began to say six or seven minutes ago, however, a curious thing about our country is the ease with which all of us—or at least everybody I know —are able to change our religions, without any noticeable damage to anything or anybody. When I was thirteen I was baptized into the Armenian Catholic Church, even though I was still singing for the Presbyterians, and even though I myself was growing a little skeptical, as it were, of the whole conventional religious pattern, and was eager, by hook or by crook, to reach an understanding of my own, and to come to terms with Omnipotence in my own way. Even after I was baptized, I carried in my heart a deep discontent.

Two months after I was baptized my voice changed, and my contract with Miss Balaifal was canceled—which was a great relief to me and a terrible blow to her.

As for the Armenian Catholic Church on Ventura Avenue, I went there only on Easter and Christmas. All the rest of the time I moved from one religion to another, and in the end was none the worse for it, so that now, like most Americans, my faith consists

in believing in every religion, including my own,
but without any ill-will toward anybody, no matter
what he believes or disbelieves, just so his personality is good.

The
Circus

Any time a circus came to town, that was all me and my old pal Joey Emerian needed to make us run hog-wild, as the saying is. All we needed to do was see the signs on the fences and in the empty store windows to start going to the dogs and neglecting our educations. All we needed to know was that a circus was on its way to town for me and Joey to start wanting to know what good a little education ever did anybody anyway.

After the circus *reached* town we were just no good at all. We spent all our time down at the trains, watching the gang unload the animals, walking out

Ventura Avenue with the lions and tigers in their golden wagons, and hanging around the grounds, trying to win the favor of the animal men, the acrobats, and the clowns.

The circus was everything everything else we knew wasn't. It was adventure, travel, danger, skill, grace, romance, comedy, peanuts, popcorn, chewing-gum and soda-water. We used to carry water to the elephants and stand around afterwards and try to seem associated with the whole magnificent affair, the putting up of the big tent, the getting of everything in order, and the worldly-wise waiting for the people to come and spend their money.

One day Joey came tearing into the classroom of the fifth grade at Emerson School ten minutes late, and without so much as removing his cap shouted, Hey, Aram, what the hell are you doing here? The circus is in town.

And sure enough I'd forgotten. I jumped up and ran out of the room with poor old Miss Flibety screaming after me, Aram Garoghlanian, you stay in this room. Do you hear me?

I heard her all right and I knew what my not staying would mean. It would mean another powerful strapping from old man Dawson. But I couldn't help it. I was just crazy about a circus.

I been looking all over for you, Joey said in the street. What happened?

I forgot. I knew it was coming all right, but I forgot it was today. How far along are they?

I was at the trains at five. I been out at the

grounds since seven. I had breakfast at the circus table, with the gang.

How are they?

Great, the same as ever. Couple more years, they told me, and I'll be ready to go away with them.

As what? Lion-tamer, or something like that?

I guess maybe not as a lion-tamer, Joey said. I figure more like a workman in the gang till I learn about being a clown or something. I don't figure I could work with lions right away.

We were out on Ventura Avenue, headed for the circus grounds, out near the County Fairgrounds, just north of the County Hospital.

What a breakfast! Joey said. Hot-cakes, ham and eggs, sausages, coffee. Boy.

Why didn't you tell me?

I thought you knew. I thought you'd be down at the trains same as last year. I would have told you if I knew you'd forgotten. What made you forget?

I don't know. Nothing, I guess.

I was wrong there, but I didn't know it at the time. I hadn't really forgotten. What I'd done was *remembered.* I'd gone to work and remembered the strapping Dawson gave me last year for staying out of school the day the circus was in town. That was the thing that had kind of kept me sleeping after four-thirty in the morning when by rights I should have been up and dressing and on my way to the trains. It was the memory of that strapping old man Dawson had given me, but I didn't know it at the time. We used to take the strappings kind of for granted, me and Joey, on account of we wanted to be fair and square with the Board of Education and if it was against the rules to stay out of school when you weren't sick, and if you were supposed to get strapped for doing it, well, there we were, we'd done it, so let the Board of Education balance things the best way they knew how. They did that with a strapping. They used to threaten to send me and Joey to Reform School but they never did it.

Circus? old man Dawson used to say. Well, bend down, boy.

So we'd bend down and old man Dawson would get some powerful shoulder exercise while we tried not to howl. We wouldn't howl for five or six licks, but after that we'd howl like Indians coming. They used to be able to hear us all over the school and old man Dawson, after our visits got to be kind of regular, urged us politely to try to make a little less noise, inasmuch as it was a school and people were trying to study.

It ain't fair to the others, he said. They're trying to learn something for themselves.

We can't help it, Joey said. It hurts.

That I know, but it seems to me there's such a thing as modulation. I believe a lad can overdo his howling if he ain't thoughtful of others. Just try to modulate that awful howl a little. I think you can do it.

He gave Joey a strapping of twenty and Joey tried his best not to howl so loud. After the strapping

Joey's face was red and old man Dawson was very tired.

How was that? Joey said.

By far the most courteous you've managed yet.

I did my best.

I'm grateful to you, old man Dawson said.

He was tired and out of breath. I moved up to the chair in front of him that he furnished during these matters to help us suffer the stinging pain. I got in the right position and he said, Wait a minute, Aram. Give a man a chance to catch his breath. I'm not twenty-three years old. I'm *sixty*-three. Let me rest a minute.

All right, but I sure would like to get this over with.

So would I, but don't howl so loud. Folks passing by in the street are liable to think this is a veritable chamber of tortures. Does it really hurt that much?

You can ask Joey.

How about it, Joey? Aren't you lads exaggerating just a little? Perhaps to impress someone in your room? Some girl, perhaps?

We don't howl to impress anybody, Mr. Dawson. Howling makes us feel ashamed, doesn't it, Aram?

It's embarrassing to go back to our seats after howling that way. We'd rather not howl if we could help it.

Well, I'll not be unreasonable. I'll only ask you to try to modulate it a little.

I'll do my best, Mr. Dawson. Catch your breath?

Give me just a moment longer.

When he got his breath back he gave me my twenty and I howled a little louder than Joey and then we went back to class. It was awfully embarrassing. Everybody was looking at us.

Well, Joey said to the class, what did you expect? You'd fall down and die if *you* got twenty. You wouldn't *howl a little*, you'd die.

That'll be enough out of you, Miss Flibety said.

Well, it's true, Joey said. They're all scared. A circus comes to town and what do they do? They come to school.

That'll be enough.

Who do they think they are, giving us dirty looks?

Miss Flibety lifted her hand, hushing Joey.

Now the circus was back in town, another year had gone by, it was April again, and we were on our way out to the grounds. Only this time it was worse than ever because they'd seen us at school and *knew* we were going out to the circus.

Do you think they'll send Stafford after us? I said. Stafford was truant officer.

We can always run, Joey said. If he comes, I'll go one way, you go another. He can't chase *both* of us.

When we got out to the grounds a couple of the little tents were up, and the big one was going up. We stood around and watched. It was great the way they did it. Just a handful of guys who looked like tramps doing work you'd think no less than a hundred men could do. Doing it with style, too.

All of a sudden a man everybody called Red hollered at me and Joey.

Here, you Arabs, give us a hand.

Me and Joey ran over to him.

Yes sir, I said.

He was a small man with very broad shoulders and very big hands. You didn't feel that he was small, because he seemed so powerful and because he had so much thick red hair on his head. You thought he was practically a giant.

He handed me and Joey a rope. The rope was attached to some canvas that was lying on the ground.

This is easy, Red said. As the boys lift the pole and get it in place you keep pulling the rope, so the canvas will go up with the pole.

Yes sir, Joey said.

Everybody was busy when we saw Stafford.

We can't run now, I said.

Let him come, Joey said. We told Red we'd give him a hand and we're going to do it.

We'll tell him we'll go with him after we get the canvas up; then we'll run.

All right, Joey said.

Stafford was a big fellow in a business suit who had a beef-red face and looked as if he ought to be a lawyer or something. He came over and said, All right, you hooligans, come along with me.

We promised to give Red a hand, Joey said. We'll come just as soon as we get this canvas up.

We were pulling for all we were worth, slipping

and falling. The men were all working hard. Red was hollering orders, and then the whole thing was over and we had done our part.

We didn't even get a chance to find out what Red was going to say to us, or if he was going to invite us to sit at the table for lunch, or what.

Joey busted loose and ran one way and I ran the other and Stafford came after *me*. I heard the circus men laughing and Red hollering, Run, boy, run. He can't catch *you*. He's soft. Give him a good run. He needs the exercise.

I could hear Stafford, too. He was very sore and he was cussing.

I got away, though, and stayed low until I saw him drive off in his Ford. Then I went back to the big tent and found Joey.

We'll get it this time, he said.

I guess it'll be Reform School.

No, it'll be thirty, and that's a lot of whacks even if he *is* sixty-three years old.

Thirty? That's liable to make me cry.

Me too, maybe, Joey said. Seems like ten can make you cry, then you hold off till it's eleven, then twelve, howling so you *won't* cry, and you think you'll start crying on the next one, but you don't. We haven't so far, anyway. Maybe we will when it's thirty, though.

Oh, well, that's tomorrow.

Red gave us some more work to do around the grounds and let us sit next to him at lunch. It was beef stew and beans, all you could eat. We talked to some acrobats who were Spanish, and to a family of Italians who worked with horses. We saw both shows, the afternoon one and the evening one, and then we helped with the work, taking the circus to pieces again; then we went down to the trains, and then home. I got home real late. In the morning I was sleepy when I had to get up for school.

They were waiting for us. Miss Flibety didn't even let us sit down for the roll call. She just told us to go to the office. Old man Dawson was waiting for us, too. Stafford was there, too, and very angry.

I figured, Well, here's where we go to Reform School.

Here they are, Mr. Dawson said to Stafford. Take them away, if you like.

It was easy to tell they'd been talking for some time and hadn't been getting along too well.

In *this* school, old man Dawson said, I do any punishing that's got to be done. Nobody else. I can't stop you from taking them to Reform School, though.

Stafford didn't say anything. He just gave old man Dawson a very dirty look and left the office.

Well, lads, old man Dawson said. How was it?

We had lunch with them, Joey said.

Good. But now down to business. What offense is this, the sixteenth or the seventeenth?

It ain't that many, Joey said. Must be eleven or twelve.

Well, I'm sure of one thing. This is the time I'm supposed to make it thirty.

I think the next one is the one you're supposed to make thirty, Joey said.

No, we've lost track somewhere, but I'm sure this is the time it goes up to thirty. Who's going to be first?

Me.

All right, Aram. Take a good hold on the chair, brace yourself, and try to modulate your howl.

Yes sir. I'll do my best, but thirty's an awful lot.

Well, a funny thing happened. He gave me thirty all right and I howled all right, but it *was* a modulated howl. It was the most modulated howl I ever howled; because it was the *easiest* strapping I ever got. I counted them and there were thirty all right, but they didn't hurt, so I didn't cry, as I was afraid I might.

It was the same with Joey. We stood together waiting to be dismissed.

I'm awfully grateful to you boys, old man Dawson said, for modulating your howls so nicely this time. I don't want people to think I'm killing you.

We wanted to thank him for giving us such easy strappings, but we didn't know how. I think he knew the way we felt, though, because he kind of laughed when he told us to go back to class.

It was a proud and happy moment for both of us because we knew everything would be all right till the County Fair opened in September.

The Three
Swimmers and the
Educated Grocer

The ditches were dry most of the year, but when they weren't dry, they were roaring. As the snows melted in the Sierra Nevadas the ditches began to roar and from somewhere, God knows where, arrived frogs and turtles, water snakes and fish. In the spring of the year the water hurried, and with it the heart, but as the fields changed from green to brown, the blossoms to fruit, the shy warmth to arrogant heat, the ditches slowed down and the heart grew lazy. The first water down the mountains and the hills was cold, swift, and frightening. It was too cold and busy to invite the naked body of a boy.

Alone, or in a group, a boy would stand on the bank of a ditch and watch the water for many minutes, and then, terribly challenged, fling off his clothes, make a running dive, come up gasping, and swim across to the other side. If the boy was the first of a group to dive, the others would soon follow, in order not to walk home in shame. It wasn't simply that the water was cold. It was more that it had no time for boys. The springtime water was as unfriendly as anything could be.

One day in April I set out for Thompson Ditch with my cousin Mourad and a pal of his named Joe Bettencourt, a Portuguese who loved nothing more than to be free and out-of-doors. A schoolroom made Joe stupid. It embarrassed him. But once out of school, once off the school-grounds, he was as intelligent, as good-natured, casual, sincere, and friendly as anyone could possibly be. As my cousin Mourad said, Joe ain't dumb—he just doesn't want an education.

It was a bright Saturday morning. We had two baloney sandwiches each, and ten cents between the three of us. We decided to walk to the ditch so that we would get there around noon, when the day would be warm. We walked along the railroad tracks to Calwa. Along the state highway to Malaga. And then east through the vineyard country to the ditch. When we said Thompson Ditch, we meant a specific place. It was an intersection of country roads, with a wooden bridge and a headgate. The swimming was south of the bridge. West of the ditch was a big fenced-in pasture, with cows and horses grazing in it. East of the ditch was the country road. The road and the ditch traveled together many miles. The flow was south, and the next bridge was two miles away. In the summer-time a day of swimming was incomplete until a boy had gone downstream to the other bridge, rested a moment in the pasture land, and then came back up, against the stream, which was a good workout.

By the time we got out to Thompson Ditch the brightness of morning had changed to a gloom that was unmistakably wintry; in fact, the beginning of a storm. The water was roaring, the sky was gray, growing black, the air was cold and unfriendly, and the landscape seemed lonely and desolate.

Joe Bettencourt said, I came all this way to swim and rain or no rain I'm going to swim.

So am I.

You wait, my cousin Mourad said. Me and Joe, we'll see how it is. If it's all right, you can come in. Can you really swim?

Aw shut up, I said.

This is what I always said when it seemed to me that somebody had unwittingly insulted me.

Well, Joe Bettencourt said, *can* you?

Sure I can swim.

If you ask *him*, my cousin Mourad said, he can do anything. Better than anybody in the world.

Neither of them knew how uncertain I was as to whether or not I could swim well enough to negotiate a dive and a swim across that body of cold roaring water. If the truth were known, when I saw the dark water roaring I was scared, challenged, and insulted.

Aw shut up, I said to the water.

I brought out my lunch and bit into one of the sandwiches. My cousin Mourad whacked my hand and almost knocked the sandwich into the water.

We eat after we swim, he said. Do you want to have cramps?

I had plumb forgotten. It was because I was so challenged and scared.

One sandwich won't give me cramps.

It'll taste better after we swim, Joe said.

He was a very kind boy. He knew I was scared and he knew I was bluffing. I knew *he* was scared, but I knew he was figuring everything out a little more wisely than I was.

Let's see, he said. We'll swim across, rest, swim back, get dressed, eat, and unless the storm passes, start for home. Otherwise we'll swim some more.

This storm isn't going to pass, my cousin Mourad said. If we're going to swim, we're going to have to do it in a hurry.

By this time Joe was taking off his clothes. My cousin Mourad was taking off his, and I was taking off mine. We stood together naked on the bank of the ditch looking at the unfriendly water. It certainly didn't invite a dive, but there was no other

honorable way to enter a body of water. If you tried
to walk in, you were just naturally not a swimmer.
If you jumped in feet first it wasn't exactly a dis-
grace, it was just bad style. On the other hand, the
water was utterly without charm, altogether unfriendly, uninviting, and sinister. The swiftness of
the water made the distance to the opposite bank
seem greater than it was.

Without a word Joe dived in. Without a word my
cousin Mourad dived in. The second or two between splashes seemed like long days dreamed in a
winter dream because I was not only scared but
very cold. With a bookful of unspoken words on my
troubled mind, I dived in.

The next thing I knew—and it wasn't more than
three seconds later—I was listening to Joe yelling,
my cousin Mourad yelling, and myself yelling.
What had happened was that we had all dived into
mud up to our elbows, had gotten free only with
great effort, and had each come up worried about
what had happened to the other two. We were all
standing in the cold roaring water, up to our knees
in soft mud.

The dives had been standing dives. If they had
been running dives we would have stuck in the
mud up to our ankles, head first, and remained
there until summer, or later.

This scared us a little on the one hand and on the
other hand made us feel lucky to be alive.

The storm broke while we stood in the mud of
the ditch.

Well, Joe said, we're going to get caught in the rain anyhow, so we might as well stay in for a while.

We were all shivering, but it seemed sensible that we should try our best to make a swim of it. The water wasn't three feet deep; nevertheless, Joe managed to leap out of the mud and swim across, and then back.

We swam for what seemed like a long time, but was probably no more than ten minutes. Then we got out of the water and mud and dressed and, standing under a tree, ate our sandwiches.

Instead of stopping, the rain increased, so we decided to set out for home right away.

We may get a ride, Joe said.

All the way to Malaga the country road was deserted. In Malaga we went into the general store and warmed ourselves at the stove and chipped in and bought a can of beans and a loaf of French bread. The proprietor of the store was a man named Darcous who wasn't a foreigner. He opened the can for us, divided the beans into three parts on three paper plates, gave us each a wooden fork, and sliced the bread for us. He was an old man who seemed funny and young.

Where you been, boys? he said.

Swimming, Joe said.

Swimming?

Sure, Joe said. We showed that river.

Well, I'll be harrowed, the grocer said. How was it?

Not three feet deep.

Cold?

Ice-cold.

Well, I'll be cultivated. Did you have fun?

Did we? Joe asked my cousin Mourad.

Joe didn't know whether it had been fun or something else.

I don't know, Mourad said. When we dived in we got stuck in the mud up to our elbows.

It wasn't easy to get loose from the mud, Joe said.

Well, I'll be pruned, the grocer said.

He opened a second can of beans, pitched an enormous forkful into his mouth, and then divided the rest onto the three paper plates.

We haven't got any more money, I said.

Now, tell me, boys, what made you do it?

Nothing, Joe said with the finality of a boy who has too many reasons to enumerate at a moment's notice, and his mouth full of beans and French bread.

Well, I'll be gathered into a pile and burned, the grocer said. Now, boys, tell me—of what race are you? Californians, or foreigners?

We're all Californians, Joe said. I was born on G Street in Fresno. Mourad here was born on Walnut Avenue or someplace on the other side of the Southern Pacific tracks, I guess, and his cousin somewhere in that neighborhood, too.

Well, I'll be irrigated. Now, tell me, boys, what sort of educations have you got?

We ain't educated, Joe said.

Well, I'll be picked off a tree and thrown into a box. Now, tell me, boys, what foreign languages do you speak?

I speak Portuguese, Joe said.

You ain't educated? I have a degree from Yale, my boy, and I can't speak Portuguese. And you, son, how about you?

I speak Armenian, my cousin Mourad said.

Well, I'll be cut off a vine and eaten grape by grape by a girl in her teens. I can't speak a word of Armenian and I'm a college graduate, class of 1892. Now, tell me, son, what's *your* name?

Aram Garoghlanian.

I think I can get it. Gar-oghlan-ian. Is that it?

That's it.

Aram.

Yes sir.

And what strange foreign language do *you* speak?

I speak Armenian, too. That's my cousin, *Mourad* Garoghlanian.

Well, I'll be harrowed, cultivated, pruned, gathered into a pile, burned, picked off a tree, and let me see what else? Thrown into a box, cut off a vine and eaten grape by grape by a girl in her teens. Yes, sir. All them things, if this doesn't beat everything. Did you encounter any reptiles?

What's reptiles? Joe said.

Snakes.

We didn't see any. The water was black.

Black water. Any fish?

Didn't see any, Joe said.

A Ford stopped in front of the store and an old man got out and came across the wood floor of the porch into the store.

Open me a bottle, Abbott, the man said.

Judge Harmon, the grocer said, I want you to meet three of the most heroic Californians of this great state.

The grocer pointed at Joe, and Joe said, Joseph Bettencourt—I speak Portuguese.

Stephen L. Harmon, the Judge said. I speak a little French.

The grocer pointed at my cousin Mourad and Mourad said, Mourad Garoghlanian.

What do you speak? the Judge said.

Armenian, my cousin Mourad said.

The grocer gave the Judge the opened bottle, the Judge lifted it to his lips, swallowed three swigs, beat his chest, and said, I'm mighty proud to meet a Californian who speaks Armenian.

The grocer pointed at me.

Aram Garoghlanian, I said.

Brothers? the Judge asked.

Cousins.

Same thing. Now, Abbott, if you please what's the occasion for this banquet and your poetic excitement, if not delirium?

These boys have just come from showing that old river, the grocer said.

The Judge took three more swigs, beat his chest three times slowly and said, Come from *what?*

They've just come from swimming.

Have any of you fevers? the Judge said.

Fever? Joe said. We ain't sick.

The grocer busted out with a roar of laughter.

Sick? he said. Judge, these boys dived naked into the black water of winter and came up glowing with the warmth of summer.

We finished the beans and the bread. We were thirsty but didn't know if we should intrude with a request for a drink of water. At least *I* didn't know, but Joe apparently didn't stop to consider.

Mr. Abbott, he said, could we have a drink of water?

Water? the grocer said. Water's for swimming in, my boy.

He fetched three paper cups, went to a small barrel with a tap, turned the tap, and filled each cup with a light golden fluid.

Here, boys. Drink. Drink the sunny juice of the golden apple, unfermented.

The Judge poured the grocer a drink out of his bottle, lifted the bottle to his lips, and said, To your health, gentlemen.

Yes sir, Joe said.

We all drank.

The Judge screwed the top onto the bottle, put the bottle into his back pocket, looked at each of us carefully, as if to remember us for the rest of his life, and said, Good-by, gentlemen. Court opens in a half hour. I must pass sentence on a man who says he *borrowed* the horse, *didn't* steal it. He speaks Mexican. The man who says he *stole* the horse speaks Italian. Good-by.

Good-by, we said.

By this time our clothes were almost dry, but the rain hadn't stopped.

Well, Joe said, thanks very much, Mr. Abbott. We've got to get home.

Not at all, the grocer said. *I* thank you.

The grocer seemed to be in a strange silence for a man who only a moment before had been so noisy with talk.

We left the store quietly and began to walk down the highway. The rain was now so light it didn't seem like rain at all. I didn't know what to make of it. Joe was the first to speak.

That Mr. Abbott, he said, he's some man.

The name on the sign is Darcous, I said. Abbott's his first name.

First or last, Joe said, he sure is some man.

That Judge was somebody too, my cousin Mourad said.

Educated, Joe said. I'd learn French myself, but who would I talk to?

We walked along the highway in silence. After a few minutes the black clouds parted, the sun came through, and away over in the east we saw the rainbow over the Sierra Nevadas.

We sure showed that old river, Joe said. Was he crazy?

I don't know, my cousin Mourad said.

It took us another hour to get home. We had all

thought about the two men and whether or not the grocer was crazy. Myself, I believed he wasn't, but at the same time it seemed to me he had acted kind of crazy.

So long, Joe said.

He went down the street. Fifty yards away he turned around and said something almost to himself.

What? my cousin Mourad shouted.

He was, Joe said.

Was what? I shouted.

Crazy.

How do you know?

How can you be cut off a vine and eaten grape by grape by a girl in her teens?

Suppose he *was* crazy? my cousin Mourad said. What of it?

Joe put his hand to his chin and began to consider. The sun was shining for all it was worth now and the world was full of light.

I don't think he was crazy, Joe shouted.

He went on down the street.

He was crazy all right, my cousin Mourad said.

Well, I said, maybe he's not always.

We decided to let the matter rest at this point until we went swimming again, at which time we would visit the store and see what happened.

A month later when, after swimming in the ditch, the three of us went into the store, the man who was in charge was a much younger man than Mr. Abbott Darcous. He wasn't a foreigner either.

What'll it be? he said.

A nickel's worth of baloney, Joe said, and a loaf of French bread.

Where's Mr. Darcous? my cousin Mourad said.

He's gone home.

Where's that?

Some place in Connecticut, I think.

We made sandwiches of the baloney and French bread and began to eat.

At last Joe asked the question.

Was he crazy?

Well, the young man said, that's hard to say. I thought he was crazy at first. Then I decided he wasn't. The way he ran this store made you think he was crazy. He gave away more than he sold. Otherwise he was all right.

Thanks, Joe said.

The store was all in order now, and a very dull place. We walked out, and began walking home.

He's crazy, Joe said.

Who? I said.

That guy in the store now, Joe said.

That young fellow?

Yeah. That new fellow in there that ain't got no education.

I think you're right, my cousin Mourad said.

All the way home we remembered the educated grocer.

Well, I'll be cultivated, Joe said when he left us and walked on down the street.

Well, I'll be picked off a tree and thrown in a box, my cousin Mourad said.

Well, I'll be cut off a vine and eaten grape by grape by a girl in her teens, I said.

He sure was some man. Twenty years later, I decided he had been a poet and had run that grocery store in that little run-down village just for the casual poetry in it instead of the paltry cash.

Locomotive 38, the Ojibway

One day a man came to town on a donkey and began loafing around in the public library where I used to spend most of my time in those days. He was a tall young Indian of the Ojibway tribe. He told me his name was Locomotive 38. Everybody in town believed he had escaped from an asylum.

Six days after he arrived in town his animal was struck by the Tulare Street trolley and seriously injured. The following day the animal passed away, most likely of internal injuries, on the corner of Mariposa and Fulton streets. The animal sank to the pavement, fell on the Indian's leg, groaned and died. When the Indian got his leg free he got up and

limped into the drug store on the corner and made
a long distance telephone call. He telephoned his
brother in Oklahoma. The call cost him a lot of
money, which he dropped into the slot as requested
by the operator as if he were in the habit of making
such calls every day.

I was in the drug store at the time, eating a Royal
Banana Special, with crushed walnuts.

When he came out of the telephone booth he saw
me sitting at the soda fountain eating this fancy
dish.

Hello, Willie, he said.

He knew my name wasn't Willie—he just liked to
call me that.

He limped to the front of the store where the gum
was, and bought three packages of Juicy Fruit. Then
he limped back and said, What is that you're eating? It looks comforting.

This is what they call a Royal Banana Special.

The Indian got up on the stool next to me.

Give me the same, he said to the soda fountain
girl.

That's too bad about your animal, I said.

There's no place for an animal in this world any
more. What kind of an automobile should I buy?

Are you going to buy an automobile?

I've been thinking about it for several minutes.

I didn't think you had any money. I thought you
were poor.

That's the impression people get. Another impression they get is that I'm crazy.

I didn't get the impression that you were crazy, but I didn't get the impression that you were rich, either.

Well, I am.

I wish I was rich.

What for?

Well, I've been wanting to go fishing at Mendota for three years in a row now. I need some equipment and some kind of an automobile to get out there in.

Can you drive an automobile? the Indian said.

I can drive anything.

Have you ever driven an automobile?

Not yet. So far I haven't had any automobile to drive, and it's against my family religion to steal an automobile.

Do you mean to tell me you believe you could get into an automobile and just start driving?

Yes sir.

Remember what I was telling you on the steps of the public library the other evening?

You mean about the machine age?

Yes.

I remember.

All right. Indians are born with an instinct for riding, rowing, hunting, fishing, and swimming. Americans are born with an instinct for fooling around with machines.

I'm no American.

I know. You're an Armenian. I remember. I asked you and you told me. You're an Armenian born in

America. You're fourteen years old and already you know you'll be able to drive an automobile the minute you get into one. You're a typical American, although your complexion, like my own, is dark.

Driving a car is no trick. There's nothing to it. It's easier than riding a donkey.

All right. Just as you say. If I go up the street and buy an automobile, will you drive for me?

Of course.

How much in wages would you want?

You mean you want to give me wages for driving an automobile?

Of course.

Well, that's very nice of you, but I don't want any money for driving an automobile.

Some of the journeys may be long ones.

The longer the better.

Are you restless?

I was born in this little old town.

Don't you like it?

I like mountains and streams and mountain lakes.

Have you ever been in the mountains?

Not yet, but I'm going to reach them some day.

I see. What kind of an automobile do you think I ought to buy?

How about a Ford roadster?

Is that the best automobile?

Do you want the *best?*

Shouldn't I have the best?

I don't know. The best costs a lot of money.

What *is* the best?

Well, some people think the Cadillac is the best. Others like the Packard. They're both pretty good. I wouldn't know which is best. The Packard is beautiful to see going down the highway, but so is the Cadillac. I've watched a lot of them fine cars going down the highway.

How much is a Packard?

Around three thousand dollars. Maybe a little more.

Can we get one right away?

I got down off the stool. He sounded crazy, but I knew he wasn't.

Listen, Mr. Locomotive, do you really want to buy a Packard right away?

You know my animal passed away a few minutes ago.

I saw it happen. They'll be arresting you any minute now.

They won't arrest me.

They will if there's a law against leaving a dead donkey in the street.

No, they won't.

Why not?

The people of this country have a lot of respect for money, and I've got a lot of money.

I guess he is crazy after all, I thought.

Where'd you get all this money?

I own some land in Oklahoma. About fifty thousand acres.

Is it worth money?

No. All but about twenty acres of it is worthless. I've got some oil wells on those twenty acres. My brother and I.

How did you Ojibways ever get down to Oklahoma? I always thought the Ojibways lived up north, around the Great Lakes.

That's right. We used to live up around the Great Lakes, but my grandfather was a pioneer. He moved west when everybody else did.

Oh. Well, I guess they won't bother you about the dead donkey then.

They won't bother me about anything. It won't be only because I've got money. It'll be also because they think I'm crazy. Nobody in this town but you knows I've got money. Do you know where we can get one of those automobiles right away?

The Packard agency is up on Broadway, just two blocks beyond the public library.

All right. If you're sure you won't mind driving for me, let's go get one of them. Something bright in color. Red, if they've got red. Where would you like to drive to first?

Would you care to go fishing at Mendota?

I'll take the ride. I'll watch you fish. Where can we get some equipment for you?

Right around the corner at Homan's.

We went around the corner to Homan's and the Indian bought twenty-seven dollars' worth of fishing equipment for me. Then we went up to the Packard agency on Broadway. They didn't have a red Packard, but there was a beautiful green one. It

was light green, the color of new grass. This was
back there in 1922. The car was a beautiful sports
touring model.

Do you really think you can drive this great big
car?

I *know* I can drive it.

The police found us in the Packard agency and
wanted to arrest the Indian for leaving the dead
donkey in the street. He showed them some papers
and the police apologized and said they'd removed
the animal and were sorry they'd troubled him
about it.

No trouble at all, he said.

He turned to the manager of the Packard agency,
Jim Lewis, who used to run for Mayor every time
election time came around.

I'll take this car, he said.

I'll draw up the papers immediately, Jim said.

What papers? I'm going to pay for it now.

You mean you want to pay three thousand two
hundred seventeen dollars and sixty-five cents *cash?*

Yes. I do. It's ready to drive, isn't it?

Of course. I'll have the boys go over it with a
cloth to take off any dust on it. I'll have them check
the motor too, and fill the gasoline tank. It won't
take more than ten minutes. If you'll step into the
office, I'll conclude the transaction immediately.

Jim and the Indian stepped into Jim's office.

About three minutes later Jim came over to me, a
man shaken to the roots.

Aram, he said, who is this guy? I thought he was

a nut. I had Johnny telephone the Pacific-Southwest and they said his bank account is being transferred from somewhere in Oklahoma. They said his account is something over a million dollars. I thought he was a nut. Do you know him?

He told me his name is Locomotive 38, I said. That's no name.

That's a translation of his Indian name, Jim said. We've got his full name on the contract. Do you know him?

I've talked to him every day since he came to town on that donkey that died this morning, but I never thought he had any money.

He says you're going to drive for him. Are you sure you're the man to drive a great big car like this, son?

Wait a minute now, Mr. Lewis, I said. Don't try to push me out of this chance of a lifetime. I can drive this big Packard as well as anybody else in town.

I'm not trying to push you out of anything. I just don't want you to drive out of here and run over six or seven innocent people and maybe smash the car. Get into the car and I'll give you a few pointers. Do you know anything about the gear shift?

I don't know anything about anything yet, but I'll soon find out.

All right. Just let me help you.

I got into the car and sat down behind the wheel. Jim got in beside me.

From now on, son, he said, I want you to regard me as a friend who will give you the shirt off his back. I want to thank you for bringing me this fine Indian gentleman.

You know I've always been crazy about driving a Packard. Now how do I do it?

Well, let's see.

He looked down at my feet.

My God, son, your feet don't reach the pedals.

Never mind that. You just explain the gear shift.

Jim explained everything while the boys wiped the dust off the car and went over the motor and filled the gasoline tank. When the Indian came out and got into the car, in the back where I insisted he should sit, I had the motor going.

He says he knows how to drive, the Indian said to Jim Lewis. By instinct. I believe him, too.

You needn't worry about Aram here, Jim said. He can drive all right. Clear the way there, boys. Let him have all the room he needs.

I turned the big car around slowly, shifted, and shot out of the agency at about fifty miles an hour, with Jim Lewis running after the car and shouting, Take it easy, son. Don't open up until you get out on the highway. The speed limit in town is twenty-five miles an hour.

The Indian wasn't at all excited, even though I was throwing him around a good deal.

I wasn't doing it on purpose, though. It was simply that I wasn't very familiar with the manner in which the automobile worked.

You're an excellent driver, Willie, he said. It's like

I said. You're an American and you were born with an instinct for mechanical contraptions like this.

We'll be in Mendota in fifteen minutes, I said. You'll see some great fishing out there.

How far is Mendota?

About thirty miles.

Thirty miles is too far to go in fifteen minutes. Take an hour. We're passing a lot of scenery I'd like to look at a little more closely.

All right, but I sure am anxious to get out there and fish.

Well, all right then, the Indian said. Go as fast as you like this time, but some time soon I'll expect you to drive a little more slowly, so I can see some of the scenery. I'm missing everything. I don't even get a chance to read the signs.

I'll travel slowly *now* if you want me to.

No. Let her go. Let her go as fast as she'll go.

Well, we got out to Mendota in half an hour. I would have made better time except for the long stretch of dirt road.

I drove the car right up to the river bank. The Indian asked if I knew how to get the top down, so he could sit in the open and watch me fish. I didn't know how to get the top down, but I got it down. It took me twenty minutes to do it.

I fished for about three hours, fell into the river twice, and finally landed a small one.

You don't know the first thing about fishing, the Indian said.

What am I doing wrong?

Everything. Have you ever fished before?

No.

I didn't think so.

What am I doing wrong?

Well, nothing in particular, only you're fishing at about the same rate of speed that you drive an automobile.

Is that wrong?

It's not exactly wrong, except that it'll keep you from getting anything to speak of, and you'll go on falling into the river.

I'm not falling. They're pulling me in. They've got an awful pull. This grass is mighty slippery, too. There ain't nothing around here to grab hold of.

I reeled in one more little one and then I asked if he'd like to go home. He said he would if I wanted to, too, so I put away the fishing equipment and the two fish and got in the car and started driving back to town.

I drove that big Packard for this Ojibway Indian, Locomotive 38, as long as he stayed in Fresno, which was all summer. He stayed at the hotel all the time. I tried to get him to learn to drive, but he said it was out of the question. I drove that Packard all over the San Joaquin Valley that summer, with the Indian in the back, chewing eight or nine sticks of gum. He told me to drive anywhere I cared to go, so it was either to some place where I could fish, or some place where I could hunt. He claimed I didn't know anything about fishing or hunting, but he was glad to see me trying. As long as I knew him he never laughed, except once. That was the time I shot at a jack-rabbit with a 12-gauge shotgun that had a terrible kick, and killed a crow. He tried to tell me all the time that that was my average. To shoot at a jack-rabbit and kill a crow. You're an American, he said. Look at the way you took to this big automobile.

One day in November his brother came to town, and the next day when I went to the hotel to get him, they told me he'd gone back to Oklahoma with his brother.

Where's the Packard?

They took the Packard, the hotel clerk said.

Who drove?

The Indian.

They're both Indians. Which of the brothers drove the car?

The one who lived at this hotel.

Are you sure?

Well, I only *saw* him get into the car out front and drive away. That's all.

Do you mean to tell me he knew how to shift gears?

It *looked* as if he did, the clerk said. He looked like an expert driver to me.

Thanks.

On the way home I figured he'd just wanted me to *believe* he couldn't drive, so *I* could drive and feel good. He was just a young man who'd come to town, bored to death or something, who'd taken advantage of the chance to be entertained by a small town kid who was bored to death, too. That's the only way I could figure it out without accepting the general theory that he was crazy.

Old Country
Advice to the American Traveler

One year my uncle Melik traveled from Fresno to New York. Before he got aboard the train his uncle Garro paid him a visit and told him about the dangers of travel.

When you get on the train, the old man said, choose your seat carefully, sit down, and do not look about.

Yes sir, my uncle said.

Several moments after the train begins to move, the old man said, two men wearing uniforms will come down the aisle and ask you for your ticket. Ignore them. They will be impostors.

How will I know?

You will know. You are no longer a child.

Yes sir.

Before you have traveled twenty miles an amiable young man will come to you and offer you a cigarette. Tell him you don't smoke. The cigarette will be doped.

Yes sir.

On your way to the diner a very beautiful young woman will bump into you intentionally and almost embrace you. She will be extremely apologetic and attractive, and your natural impulse will be to cultivate her friendship. Dismiss your natural impulse and go on in and eat. The woman will be an adventuress.

A what? my uncle said.

A whore, the old man shouted. Go on in and eat. Order the best food, and if the diner is crowded, and the beautiful young woman sits across the table from you, do not look into her eyes. If she speaks, pretend to be deaf.

Yes sir.

Pretend to be deaf, the old man said. That is the only way out of it.

Out of what?

Out of the whole ungodly mess. I have traveled. I know what I'm talking about.

Yes sir.

Let's say no more about it.

Yes sir.

Let's not speak of the matter again. It's finished. I have seven children. My life has been a full and righteous one. Let's not give it another thought. I have land, vines, trees, cattle, and money. One cannot have everything—except for a day or two at a time.

Yes sir.

On your way back to your seat from the diner, the old man said, you will pass through the smoker. There you will find a game of cards in progress. The players will be three middle-aged men with expensive-looking rings on their fingers. They will nod at you pleasantly and one of them will invite you to join the game. Tell them, No speak English.

Yes sir.

That is all.

Thank you very much, my uncle said.

One thing more, the old man said. When you go to bed at night, take your money out of your pocket and put it in your shoe. Put your shoe under your pillow, keep your head on the pillow all night, *and don't sleep.*

Yes sir.

That is all.

The old man went away and the next day my uncle Melik got aboard the train and traveled straight across America to New York. The two men in uniforms were not impostors, the young man with the doped cigarette did not arrive, the beautiful young woman did not sit across the table from him in the diner, and there was no card game in progress in the smoker. My uncle put his money in his shoe and put his shoe under his pillow and put his head on the pillow and didn't sleep all night the first night, but the second night he abandoned the whole ritual.

The second day he *himself* offered another young man a cigarette which the other young man accepted. In the diner my uncle went out of his way to sit at a table with a young lady. He started a poker game in the smoker, and long before the train ever got to New York my uncle knew everybody aboard the train and everybody knew him. Once, while the train was traveling through Ohio, my uncle and the young man who had accepted the cigarette and two young ladies on their way to Vassar formed a quartette and sang *The Wabash Blues*.

The journey was a very pleasant one.

When my uncle Melik came back from New York, his old uncle Garro visited him again.

I see you are looking all right, he said. Did you follow my instructions?

Yes sir, my uncle said.

The old man looked far away in space.

I am pleased that *someone* has profited by my experience, he said.

The Poor
and Burning
Arab

My uncle Khosrove, himself a
man of furious energy and uncommon sorrow, had
for a friend one year a small man from the old
country who was as still as a rock inwardly, whose
sadness was expressed by brushing a speck of dust
from his knee and never speaking.

This man was an Arab named Khalil. He was no
bigger than a boy of eight, but, like my uncle Khos-

rove, had a very big mustache. He was probably in his early sixties. In spite of his mustache, however, he impressed one as being closer to a child in heart than to a man. His eyes were the eyes of a child, but seemed to be full of years of remembrance—years and years of being separated from things deeply loved, as perhaps his native land, his father, his mother, his brother, his horse, or something else. The hair on his head was soft and thick, and as black as black ever was, and parted on the left side, the way small boys who had just reached America from the old country were taught by their parents to part their hair. His head was, in fact, the head of a schoolboy, except for the mustache, and so was his body, except for the broad shoulders. He could speak no English, only a little Turkish, a few words of Kurdish, and only a few of Armenian, but he hardly ever spoke anyway. When he did, he spoke in a voice that seemed to come not so much from himself as from the old country. He spoke, also, as if he regretted the necessity to do so, as if it were pathetic for one to try to express what could never be expressed, as if anything he might say would only add to the sorrow already existing in himself.

How he won the regard of my uncle Khosrove, a man who *had* to say *something* at least, is a thing none of us ever learned. Little enough is learned from people who are always talking, let alone from people who hardly ever talk, except, as in the case of my uncle Khosrove, to swear or demand that someone else stop talking. My uncle Khosrove prob- ably met the Arab at the Arax Coffee House.

He picked his friends and enemies from the way they played *tavli,* which in this country is known as backgammon. Games of any sort are tests of human behavior under stress, and, even though my uncle Khosrove himself was probably the worst loser in the world, he despised any other man who lost without grace.

What are you grieving about? he would shout at such a loser. It's a game, isn't it? Do you lose your life with it?

He himself lost *his* life when he lost a game, but it was inconceivable to him that anyone else might regard the symbols of the game as profoundly as he did. To the others the game was *only* a game, as far as he was concerned. To himself, however, the game was destiny—over a board on a table, with an insignificant man across the table rattling the dice, talking to them in Turkish, coaxing them, whisper- ing, shouting, and in many other ways humiliating himself.

My uncle Khosrove, on the other hand, despised the dice, regarded them as his personal enemies, and never spoke to them. He threw them out of the window or across the room, and pushed the board off the table.

The sons of dogs! he would shout.

And then, pointing furiously at his opponent, he would shout, And you! My own countryman! You are not ashamed. You debase yourself before them.

You pray to them. I am ashamed for you. I spit on the sons of dogs.

Naturally, no one ever played a game of *tavli* with my uncle Khosrove twice.

The Arax Coffee House was a place of great fame and importance in its day. In this day it is the same, although many have died who went there twenty years ago.

For the most part the place was frequented by Armenians, but others came, too. All who remembered the old country. All who loved it. All who had played *tavli* and the card game *scambile* in the old country. All who enjoyed the food of the old country, the wine, the *rakhi*, and the small cups of coffee in the afternoons. All who loved the songs, and the stories. And all who liked to be in a place with a familiar smell, thousands of miles from home.

Most of the time my uncle Khosrove reached this place around three in the afternoon. He would stand a moment looking over the men, and then sit down in a corner, alone. He usually sat an hour, without moving, and then would go away, terribly angry, although no one had said a word to him.

Poor little ones, he would say. Poor little orphans. Or, literally, Poor and burning orphans.

Poor and burning—it's impossible to translate this one. Nothing, however, is more sorrowful than the *poor and burning* in life and in the world.

Most likely, sitting in the Arax Coffee House one day, my uncle Khosrove noticed the little Arab, and knew him to be a man of worth. Perhaps the man had been seated, playing *tavli,* his broad shoulders over the board, his child's head somber and full of understanding and regret, and perhaps after the game my uncle Khosrove had seen him get up and stand, no bigger than a child.

It may even be that the man came to the Coffee House and, not knowing my uncle Khosrove, played a game of *tavli* with him and *lost,* and did not complain; and, in fact, understood *who* my uncle Khosrove was—without being told. It may even be that the Arab did not pray to the dice.

Whatever the source of their friendship, whatever the understanding between the two, and whatever the communion they shared, they were at any rate together occasionally in our parlor, and welcome.

The first time my uncle Khosrove brought the Arab to our house, he neglected to introduce him. My mother assumed that the Arab was a countryman of ours, perhaps a distant cousin, although he was a little darker than most of the members of our tribe, and smaller. Which, of course, was no matter; nothing more than the charm of a people; the variety; the quality which made them human and worthy of further extension in time.

The Arab sat down that first day only after my mother had asked him a half-dozen times to be at home.

Was he deaf? she thought.

No, it was obvious that he could hear; he listened so intently.

Perhaps he didn't understand our dialect. My mother asked what city he was from. He did not reply, except to brush dust from the sleeve of his coat. Then in Turkish my mother said, Are you an Armenian? This the Arab understood; he replied in Turkish that he was an Arab.

A poor and burning little orphan, my uncle Khosrove whispered.

For a moment my mother imagined that the Arab might wish to speak, but it was soon obvious that, like my uncle Khosrove, nothing grieved him more than to do so. He could, if necessary, speak, but there was simply nothing, in all truth, to say.

My mother took the two men tobacco, and coffee, and motioned to me to leave.

They want to talk, she said.

Talk? I said.

They want to be alone.

I sat at the table in the dining room and began turning the pages of a year-old copy of the *Saturday Evening Post* that I knew by heart—especially the pictures: Jello, very architectural; automobiles, with high-toned people standing around; flashlights flashing into dark places; tables set with bowls of soup steaming; young men in fancy ready-made suits and coats; and all sorts of other pictures.

I must have turned the pages a little too quickly, however.

My uncle Khosrove shouted, Quiet, boy, quiet.

I looked into the parlor just in time to see the Arab brush dust from his knee.

The two men sat in the parlor an hour, and then the Arab breathed very deeply through his nose and without a word left the house.

I went into the parlor and sat where he had sat. What's his name? I said.

Quiet, my uncle Khosrove said.

Well, what's his name? I said again.

My uncle Khosrove was so irritated he didn't know what to do. He called out to my mother, as if he were being murdered.

Mariam! he shouted. Mariam!

My mother hurried into the parlor.

What is it? she said.

Send him away—please, my uncle Khosrove said.

Why? What's the matter?

He wants to know the Arab's name.

Well, all right. He's a child. He's curious. Tell him.

I see, my uncle Khosrove groaned. You, too. My own sister. My own poor and burning little sister.

Well, what *is* the Arab's name?

I won't tell. That's all. I won't tell.

He got up and left the house.

He doesn't know the man's name, my mother explained. And you've got no business irritating him.

Three days later when my uncle Khosrove and the Arab came to our house I was in the parlor.

My uncle Khosrove came straight to me and said, His name is Khalil. Now go away.

I left the house and waited in the yard for one of

my cousins to arrive. After ten minutes, nobody arrived, so I went to my cousin Mourad's house and spent an hour arguing with him about which of us would be the stronger in five years. We wrestled three times and I lost three times, but once I *almost* won.

When I got home the two men were gone. I ran straight to the parlor from the back of the house, but they weren't there. The only thing in the room was their smell and the smell of tobacco smoke.

What did they talk about? I asked my mother.

I didn't listen.

Did they talk at all?

I don't know.

They didn't.

Some people talk when they have something to say, my mother said, and some people don't.

How can you talk if you don't say anything?

You talk without words. We are always talking without words.

Well, what good are words, then?

Not very good, most of the time. Most of the time they're only good to keep back what you really want to say, or something you don't want known.

Well, do *they* talk?

I think they do. They sit and sip coffee and smoke cigarettes. They never open their mouths, but they're talking all the time. They understand one another and don't need to open their mouths. They have nothing to keep back.

Do they really know what they're talking about?

Of course.

Well, what is it? I said.

I can't tell you, my mother said, because it isn't in words; but they know.

For a year my uncle Khosrove and the Arab came to our house every now and then and sat in the parlor. Sometimes they sat an hour, sometimes two.

Once my uncle Khosrove suddenly shouted at the Arab, *Pay no attention to it, I tell you,* although the Arab had said nothing.

But most of the time nothing at all was said until it was time for them to go. Then my uncle Khosrove would say quietly, The poor and burning orphans, and the Arab would brush dust from his knee.

One day when my uncle Khosrove came to our house alone, I realized that the Arab had not visited our house in several months.

Where is the Arab? I said.

What Arab? my uncle Khosrove said.

That poor and burning little Arab that used to come here with you. Where is he?

Mariam! my uncle Khosrove shouted. He was standing, terrified.

Oh-oh, I thought. What have I done now?

Mariam! Mariam!

My mother came into the parlor.

What is it? she said.

If you please, my uncle Khosrove said. He is your son. You are my little sister. Please send him away. I love him with all my heart. He is an American. He was born here. He will be a great man some day. I have no doubt about it. Please send him away.

Why, what is it?

What is it? He talks. He asks questions. I love him.

Aram, my mother said.

I was standing too, and if my uncle Khosrove was angry at me, I was angrier at him.

Where is the Arab? I shouted.

My uncle Khosrove pointed me out to my mother —with despair. There you are, his gesture said. Your son. My nephew. My own flesh and blood. You see? We are all poor and burning orphans. All except *him.*

Aram, my mother said.

Well, if you don't talk, I can't understand. *Where is the Arab?*

My uncle Khosrove left the house without a word.

The Arab is dead, my mother said.

When did he tell you?

He didn't tell me.

Well, how did you find out?

I don't know how, but he is dead.

My uncle Khosrove didn't visit our house again for many days. For a while I thought he would *never* come back. When he came at last he stood in the parlor with his hat on his head and said, The Arab is dead. He died an orphan in an alien world, six thousand miles from home. He wanted to go home and die. He wanted to see his sons again. He wanted to talk to them again. He wanted to smell them. He wanted to hear them breathing. He had no money. He used to think about them all the time. Now go away. I love you.

I wanted to ask some more questions, especially about the Arab's sons, how many there were, how long he had been away from them, and so on, but I decided I would rather visit my cousin Mourad and see if I couldn't hold him down *now*, so I went away without saying a word—which most likely pleased my uncle Khosrove very much, and made him feel maybe there was some hope for me, after all.

A
Word to Scoffers

From Reno to Salt Lake City all you get to see from a bus or any other kind of conveyance is desert, and in August all you feel is dry heat. Desert is sand spread out evenly in every direction, different kinds of cactus, and the sun. Sometimes the sand looks white, sometimes brown, and around sundown the color of the sand changes from white or brown to yellow, and then black. Then it is night, and that is when the desert is best of all. When the desert and night join one another you get what amounts to silence.

This is a thing you remember.

The remembrance is full of the hush and mystery of the world.

I know all this because I rode in a bus from Reno to Salt Lake City once, on my way to New York.

My uncle Gyko told me to get out of town and go to New York. He said, Don't stay in these little town. Go to Nor York. I tell you, Aram, eat ease eansanity to stay here.

That's how it happened that I rode in the bus from Reno to Salt Lake City.

That was country I had never seen, or even imagined. Wide dry waste-land, full of nothing. I kept my eyes open night and day watching that country. I didn't want to pass through country like that without finding out all I could about it.

The bus left Reno a little after midnight. Reno is one of those American towns that lives on nothing but the disease of people. The only thing there is gambling and whoring.

Consequently, the city lights are bright.

I remember going into a gambling joint and seeing clearly all the way from the rail to the poker game in the corner of the room the three black hairs growing out of the dealer's nose. It was that light.

Then the bus rolled out of Reno into the desert. That was a mighty remarkable difference to dwell upon: first the bright lights of the gambling joints of Reno, and then the desert at night. I dwelt on those bright lights and the desert from midnight till morning, and even then I didn't find out enough for one small sentence of three words.

All I did in the morning was yawn. When the bus stopped, I got out and had a good look. Well, all it was was dirt and sky, and the sun coming up. I couldn't think of three little words with which to clarify the situation. It was nothing. That's all. Nothing at all. No streets, no buildings, no corners, no doorways, no doors, no windows, no signs, nothing.

My uncle Gyko told me not to stay in a small town like the small town I was born in, and now I couldn't wait to get out of the desert into a big town and be able to understand something again. I began to figure it wouldn't do my uncle Gyko any harm to get out of our small town and pass through the desert himself. I figured he might not be so sure about everything if he got himself all surrounded by the desert, day and night, and felt that sullen silence. My uncle Gyko hadn't read as many smart books as I had read because he read slower and with greater difficulty, but he had read everything he had read very carefully and memorized whole pages of the works of writers who had lived in Europe as long as two hundred years ago. In his own broken-English way he used to cut loose with a lot of derivative invective. He used to call people sheep, and claim that he himself wasn't a sheep. I myself was just as wise as my uncle Gyko, only I didn't speak with an accent. My uncle Gyko said, Get out of these town and go to Nor York.

I figured my uncle Gyko ought to visit the desert himself and see how *he* felt. I figured I couldn't figure out anything in a place so empty as all that. I didn't feel like feeling smart at all. I felt lonely, too. That's why I tried to start a conversation with the only girl on the bus, inexperienced as I was in the art of polite conversation.

What's the name of this place? I said to the girl.

She was at least thirty-five and ugly.

What place?

All this land around here.

I don't know, the girl said.

That was as far as the conversation went until late the next afternoon when the girl asked me what time it was and I said I didn't know.

I didn't even know what day it was. I was beginning to find out that all I knew was that I didn't know anything, and all I wanted was to get to Salt Lake City as soon as possible so I could see streets and places again and people walking around, and maybe get back my tremendous book-learning that was so useless in the desert.

Just let me get to a city again, I thought, and I'll be as smart as the next fellow. Maybe smarter. Just get me out of this desolation and I'll start throwing wise cracks all over the place.

Well, I was wrong. When I got to Salt Lake City I felt more confused than ever. I couldn't find a room for fifty cents, or a restaurant where I could get a big dinner for fifteen cents. I felt tired and hungry and sleepy and sore at the people in the streets, and the buildings there, and I wished to Christ I hadn't left home.

I paid a dollar for a little room in an old hotel.

The room turned out to be haunted. It was the toughest room I ever tried to stay in, but I used to be very stubborn in those days and I stayed in the room until I could see every kind of evil form that never in the history of the world reached material substance, and could hear every kind of awful sound that science insisted didn't exist. I was scared stiff. In two hours I didn't move from the rocking-chair in the middle of the room because I was sure something would grab hold of me and strangle me before I could get to the door or window. The room was full of evil things. I don't know how I got out of it alive, but I got out all right.

I walked through the streets of Salt Lake City and found a restaurant where you could get a hamburger dinner for a quarter.

After dinner, I went back to that little room in that little hotel and got in bed without taking off any of my clothes, not even my shoes or my hat. I wanted to be ready to sprint in case of riot, fire, earthquake, flood, pestilence, or any other kind of emergency. Before turning out the light I practiced getting out of the bed and getting to the door. I was making it in one jump to the door.

I got up at five in the morning because I didn't want to miss the bus that was leaving town at half past nine.

At a quarter past nine I was standing in front of the bus depot, smoking a five cent cigar, trying to get back my young irreligious poise so that I could be happy again when a very tall and melancholy-looking man of fifty in overalls handed me a little pamphlet and said, Son, are you saved?

I had never before seen such a melancholy-looking man. Six feet two or three, no more than a hundred and twenty pounds in weight, unshaved, and full of religion. I figured he was going to ask me for a dime because he looked more like a hungry tramp than a holy man, but all he did was hand me the religious pamphlet and ask if I was saved. The title of the story on the pamphlet was *A Word to Scoffers*, and the missionary had found his man all right. I didn't know. I couldn't tell at the time. I was all mixed up.

I took a sophisticated puff on the nickel cigar and said, No, I don't think I'm saved, but I'm sympathetic.

Brother, said the religious man, I can save you through the gospel of Brigham Young.

I'm leaving town in fifteen minutes.

That's all right. I once saved a man in four minutes.

What do I have to do?

Son, you don't have to do anything. You have no idea how close to being saved every man alive is. Any man you can think of. I used to be something of a rounder myself, snappy clothes, strong drink, panatela cigars, cards, dice, horses, sporting girls. Everything. Changed over-night.

Why?

Lost my luck and couldn't sleep. Fell to thinking

and found out I never was intended to be an enemy of the truth.

What truth?

God's *holy* truth. No man is ever much of an enemy of the truth. All them crazy things people do is because they don't know what they're after.

Well, what *are* they after?

Truth. Every man who cheats at cards, carries on with women, holds up a bank, gets drunk, or travels, is looking for truth. I guess you're going somewhere, son. Where you going?

I'm on my way to New York.

Well, you won't find any truth there. I been there six times in the last thirty years. You can go hopping around all over the world and never find out anything because that ain't the way you find out anything. All you got to do is change your attitude.

That ought to be easy.

Easiest thing in the world.

I'm game. I've got nothing to lose. How do I change my attitude?

Well, said the religious man, you stop trying to figure things out and you *believe*.

Believe? Believe *what*?

Why, everything. Everything you can think of, left, right, north, east, south, west, upstairs, downstairs and all around, inside, out, visible, invisible, good and bad and neither and both. That's the little secret. Took me fifty years to find out.

Is that all I have to do?

That's all, son.

O.K., *I believe.*

Son, said the religious man, you're saved. You can go to New York now or anywhere else, and everything will be smooth and easy.

I hope you're right.

You'll find out.

The big bus came to the curb and I got in. The lanky man of God came to the window, smiling proudly.

You're the fifty-seventh man I've saved, he said.

Well, so long. And thanks for the little secret.

Glad to do it. Don't forget. Just believe.

I won't forget. I'll believe.

Anything, he said.

The motor of the bus started.

Any old thing at all, I said.

The bus belched smoke and slowly rolled away.

I thought I was kidding the old padre of Salt Lake City, getting back my vast book-learning and antireligious poise, but I was sadly mistaken, because unwittingly I *had* been saved. In less than ten minutes after the bus left Salt Lake City I was believing everything, left and right, as the missionary had said, and it's been that way with me ever since.

ABOUT THE AUTHOR

William Saroyan was born in Fresno, California, in 1908 of Armenian parentage. He received the Pulitzer Prize for Drama in 1940 for *The Time of Your Life* and wrote many short stories, plays and novels including *The Daring Young Man on the Flying Trapeze* (1934), *My Heart's in the Highlands* (1939) and *The Human Comedy* (1943). His love of people and of America produced some of the most sympathetic and wildly uninhibited literature of our time.